"a terrifying adventure...Grim is a truly villainous character." - *Books for Keeps*

"All the frosty bearded splendour of the Norse sagas condensed into a fun, thrilling tale for kids with a taste for high adventure...tipped to be a best-selling series." - *www.waterstones.com (5-star Covent Garden bookseller review)*

"This series just keeps getting better and better! Grim Gruesome is a truly nasty villain, from his completely gross scabbed and pussed over finger stump to his taste for children boiled or raw! With plenty of historical detail thrown in, this is a well put together and wonderfully told romp." - *www.waterstones.com (4-star York bookseller review)*

"An outstanding action packed historical novel, keeping you tense and on edge" - *Imogen, 10*
"The most gripping novel since Lord of the Rings" - *Ben, 8*
"A truly thrilling story" - *Megan, 11*
"A brilliant book...adventurous, exciting and action packed" - *Uji, 11*   *All members of York Children's Book Group*

"a corking yarn which is both fast and exciting." - *Adele Geras*

"It races from page to page." - *The Journal*

"Boys and air̶ ̶ ̶ ̶ ̶ ̶ ̶ ̶ ̶ ̶ ̶ ̶ ̶ sharing in their despair (̶ ̶ ̶ ̶   ̶.org.uk

GRIM GRUESOME
VIKING VILLAIN

in

THE QUEEN'S POISON

ROSALIND KERVEN

www.grimgruesome.com

First published in the UK by Talking Stone 2009

Text copyright © Rosalind Kerven 2009
Illustrations copyright © David Wyatt 2008, 2009

Talking Stone
an author-led publishing team
Swindonburn Cottage West, Sharperton
Morpeth, Northumberland, NE65 7AP

Printed and bound by CPI Antony Rowe, Chippenham, Wiltshire

ISBN: 978-0-9537454-4-9

A big thank you to my fantastic publishing team:

Editor: Helen Greathead

Designer: Alison Gadsby

Artist: David Wyatt

Collect the whole series of books about

GRIM GRUESOME
Viking Villain:

THE CURSED SWORD

THE QUEEN'S POISON

coming soon:
TROLL'S TREASURE

THE NORTH LANDS
A THOUSAND YEARS AGO
THE VIKING AGE

Come back through time to
the Viking town of Jorvik!

Jorvik was the heart of a Viking kingdom
that sprawled across northern England.
It was a maze of close-packed, wooden houses where
Viking and English people lived uneasily side by side.
Day and night the winding streets bustled with
merchants, pigs, storytellers, housewives, mice,
sword-makers, sailors, cats, nobles, foreigners,
jewellers, children, woodcarvers, geese,
musicians, soldiers, dogs and beggars.
The whole place stank
of sewage, ships' tar and wood-smoke.

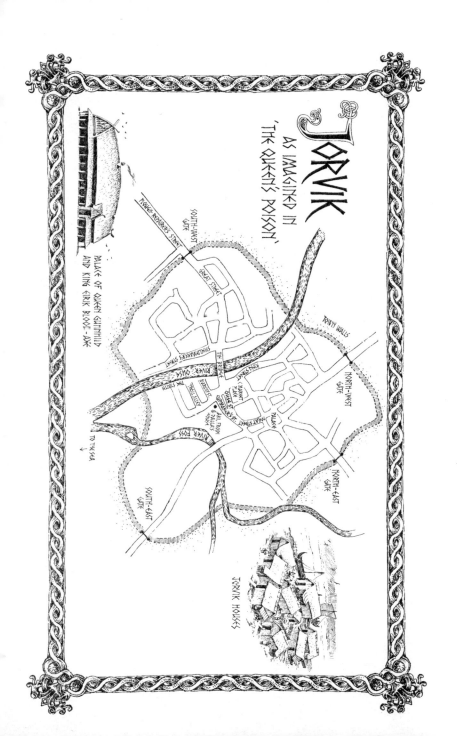

JORVIK
AS IMAGINED IN
'THE QUEEN'S POISON'

TOWER REPAIRERS STREET

SOUTH-WEST GATE

PALACE OF QUEEN GUNNHILD
AND KING EIRIK BLOOD-AXE

GREAT STREET

SHIELDMAKERS STREET

RIVER OUSE

TOWN WALLS

THE BRIDGE

KING'S SQUARE

MARKET PLACE

NORTH-WEST GATE

THE SMITH

JORVIK MINSTER

KIRKGATE

JARL THORIR'S HOUSE

GUNNAR'S HOUSE

COAT STREET

PALACE

RIVER FOSS

TO THE SEA

NORTH-EAST GATE

SOUTH-EAST GATE

JORVIK HOUSES

1

It was a dark and stormy autumn morning at the end of Slaughtering Month. A biting wind was blowing over the Viking kingdom. The sky crackled with thunder and rain lashed down in sheets.

Only a fool would go out in such weather! So why on earth was a lone horseman galloping along the road that led from the forest?

The horseman stopped at a heavy iron gate in the towering wall that surrounded Jorvik. A watchman peered out suspiciously from the shelter of its arch.

'What do you want, on a day like this?' he called.

The rider shouted back in a rasping voice: 'You must take a message for me!'

'Oh, must I now?' retorted the watchman. 'Who's it for, stranger?'

'Thora,' the horseman answered. The rain streamed

over his hood and cloak, turning him dark and smooth as a whale.

'Which Thora, stranger?'

'The one who's married to Snorri the bucket-maker,' said the horseman. He made a curious snorting noise in his throat. 'You must know her: she has three children, all with red hair. Hurry, man, hurry! It's a matter of life and death!'

'Oh, *her*,' said the watchman. 'Poor woman, her two sons are fine enough lads, but that daughter of hers is a right terror. What's the message, stranger?'

The horseman reached into his cloak with a gloved hand and pulled out a strip of wood. It was thickly carved with dark, spiky lines: rune letters. He leaned down from his horse and pressed it through the bars of the gate into the watchman's grasp.

Then he turned and galloped away.

The rain teemed down. Lightening zigzagged across the sky. The man and his horse were dark as midnight. But the horse's tail, flying in the wind, was touched with unearthly light.

The watchman stared after them and shrugged. He examined the rune-stick. But as he couldn't read, he didn't have a clue what it said.

2

The watchman slipped the rune-stick into the battered leather pouch that dangled from his belt. Then he wrapped his thick, grey cloak tightly round him to keep out the rain and set off, grumbling, on his errand.

Luckily, it wasn't far from the gate to Cupmaker's Street where Thora and her husband Snorri the bucket-maker lived. By the time the watchman turned the corner into their street, the storm had already blown away.

The place was bustling. Shopkeepers were busy setting up tables in the storm puddles in front of their houses, and spreading them with home-made goods to sell. Several stalls sold the wooden cups that gave the street its name. Others offered jewellery, combs, fish, shoes, knives, bales of cloth, goose and chicken eggs, embroidered ribbons, swords and toys. Housewives and children were swarming around them.

The watchman elbowed his way through them and up the slope to the last house. The stall in front of it was stacked with wooden buckets. A young girl with straggly, long red hair was standing guard beside it, scratching the flea bites on her legs.

'Hey, lass!' called the watchman. 'You're Dalla, aren't you? And your pa's Snorri the bucket-maker?'

The girl giggled and nodded.

The watchman pulled out the rune-stick.

'Go and give this to your mam at once,' he said. 'Tell her I got it from a mysterious stranger. Come on, get a move on – he said it was really urgent!'

3

'Mam!' yelled Dalla. 'MAM!'

She ran into the little, one-roomed house. It was one of the older buildings in Jorvik, built of wattle and daub. It was cramped and crowded, with two built-in wall-benches, storage chests, jars, pots and a big weaving-loom at one end. There were no windows, but it was cheerfully lit by lamplight and a flickering fire. The floor was covered with sawdust.

Thora, Dalla's mother, was squatting by the stone-edged fire-pit in the centre, stirring a steaming pot.

'Aw, you made me jump out of my skin, you naughty girl!' she cried, jumping up. 'What's the matter? Is it a customer?'

'A watchman gave me this for you,' said Dalla, 'from a mystery horseman – it's urgent!'

Thora wiped her hands on her long, grubby apron

and tucked some stray hair under her headscarf. She took the rune-stick and peered at it.

'Runes!' she grumbled. 'I can't make any sense of these. We'll have to ask your pa.'

Dalla followed her mother outside, into the long yard at the back. The storm had turned it into a muddy quagmire. The family's chickens were pecking at it miserably, looking very bedraggled. Snorri was standing at his worktable, busily sawing away. Dalla's two older brothers, Aki and Frodi, were helping him.

'Can you tell us what this says, Snorri?' said Thora. 'It's come from a mystery horseman.'

Snorri took the rune-stick and peered at it, scratching his head.

'Who in Thor's name would send *you* a rune message?' he said. 'Eh, I've clean forgotten how to read these things, you know… Hold on though, Thora my love, that first word looks familiar. I reckon it's your sister's name, Jorunn.'

'Aunty Jorunn!' cried Frodi. 'Whatever's she up to?'

'Give it here, Mam,' said Aki. He was the older boy – already tall and strong. 'I can read runes.'

Snorri nudged Thora. 'Our Aki's a right clever one,' he said admiringly.

Aki flushed with pride and took the rune-stick. Frodi stood on tiptoe and peered over his shoulder. Aki traced his fingers over the carvings and slowly spelled out the words:

ᛁᚠᚱᚢᚾ : ᛘᛁᛏ : ᚦᛁᛋ : ᚱᚢᛏᛋ : ᚠᛅᛦ : ᚦᛅᚱᛋ

'JORUNN MADE THESE RUNES FOR THORA

ᛁ : ᛏᛘ : ᚠᛏᚱᛁ : ᛁᛚ

I AM VERY ILL

ᛁ : ᛏᚱᛋᛒᛏᛘ : ᛏᚢ : ᛏᛁ

I EXPECT TO DIE

ᚱᚢᛘ : ᛏᚠ : ᛘᛁ : ᚱᚢᛁᚱᛏᛁ

COME TO ME QUICKLY'

Thora turned white. She sat down heavily.

'Mighty Thor!' she cried. 'Goddess Freyja's amber tears! My poor darling sister! Dying! Snorri – I've got to go to her at once!'

'Of course,' said Snorri soothingly.

Thora dabbed her eyes with the hem of her apron. 'But she lives right on the other side of the kingdom!' she wailed. 'I can't travel all that way on my own – not over the high hills and through miles of forest! There'll be wolves – and robbers!'

'Don't worry,' said Snorri. 'I'll come with you.'

'But what about the children?' cried Thora. 'They'll have to come too.'

'We can't afford that,' said Snorri. 'It'll cost a fortune to hire horses for all five of us.'

'But who will look after them?' wailed Thora. 'Oh, oh! If only we had some kinsfolk nearby. I knew it was a mistake moving here to Jorvik, with all our relations so far away. We can't leave the children on their own!'

'Well...' said Snorri slowly, 'if you want to see your sister before she dies, my love, it looks like we'll have to. But it's not so terrible. Our Aki's a big, sensible lad – you can hardly call him a child – I mean, he's nearly fourteen. Look at all that bum-fluff on his chin: his beard's really starting to grow! He's plenty old enough to look after the other two for a few days.'

Aki stood up straight. He plumped out his chest.

'Of course I am,' he said. 'Don't worry, Mam, I'll keep Frodi and Dalla safe while you go and see Aunty Jorunn. Don't forget I won the lads' wrestling match at Midsummer Feast. And I reckon I can look after the shop for you as well.'

Snorri beamed proudly at him.

'Well I'm sure *you'll* be all right,' said Thora doubtfully. 'And Frodi too: you're growing into a fine lad like Aki, aren't you Frodi?'

Snorri nodded at his younger son.

'But it's naughty little Dalla I'm worried about,' said Thora. 'Just look at her!'

Dalla was standing at the worktable, using a chisel to scoop a pile of sawdust into a miniature mountain. Thora slapped her hand away.

'Stop fiddling with your father's tools, you good-for-nothing girl!' she scolded. 'And by the way, why haven't you done your spinning this morning? You've been larking round town again, haven't you!'

Dalla grinned at her mischievously.

'Tut-tut,' said Snorri.

'Aw,' scolded Thora, 'she drives me mad, she does. Are you sure you can cope with her, Aki? You know she can't keep her hands out of mischief...'

4

By early next morning, everything was arranged. Thora had given the boys a long list of instructions. The most important was to keep Dalla out of trouble. Snorri had given them enough silver pennies to buy food while they were away – hidden safely in an innocent-looking pot behind the clothes chest.

Snorri and Thora hugged Dalla, and slapped the boys' shoulders fondly. Then they waved goodbye, fetched their hired horses, and set off for Jorunn's farm in the far west of the kingdom.

As soon as they had gone, Aki and Frodi fetched their saws and hammers and went to the door.

'Where are you going with those?' asked Dalla.

'Out to the yard of course,' said Aki. 'We promised Pa we'd nail up some more buckets while he's away.'

'Aw, you goody-goodies!' cried Dalla. 'Do it later! Let's go out instead – have some fun!'

'Well…' said Frodi.

'Not until we've done some work,' said Aki firmly. 'Anyway Dalla, Mam said *you* have to get on with your spinning, didn't she?'

'I am NOT doing my spinning!' said Dalla. 'You know I always get it tangled – I hate it!' She picked up her spindle from the shelf where it lay in a mess of grubby raw wool, and tossed it carelessly into a corner. 'Goose poo to that! Come on, let's make the most of being on our own! Why don't we go and see what's happening down the Staith?'

The Staith was a wooden-paved area beside the River Ouse, right in the centre of town. It was a mooring place for all the ships and boats that sailed up and down between Jorvik and the sea.

'You're not allowed down there, are you Dalla?' said Frodi sharply.

'Definitely not,' said Aki.

Dalla giggled. 'So what? I don't care about Mam and Pa's stupid rules. I often go to the Staith.'

'Well, Mam says it's not a safe place for girls,' said Aki, 'and I reckon she's right, with all those foreign

21

sailors hanging around there. They're usually drunk out of their minds, and they talk really crude...'

'I know, I've seen them,' said Dalla. 'And heard them! There's often gangs of ruffians having sword fights. They're so exciting!'

'You stupid girl,' said Aki. 'People get killed!'

'Well, no one's ever tried to kill *me*,' said Dalla. 'And I love seeing those big ships from over the sea, and all the fancy foreign things that get unloaded off them.'

'Mam'll lock you up if she finds out what you get up to!' said Aki. 'Don't you dare go down the Staith while *I'm* in charge, Dalla. I can't risk you...'

'There won't be any risk if we all go down there *together*,' grinned Dalla. 'I'll be perfectly safe – no one ever messes with you, Aki, do they? And...and...then I promise I'll stay home for the rest of the day and not annoy you at all.'

Aki sighed.

'She won't stop nagging until we take her,' said Frodi.

'That's right,' grinned Dalla. 'But I promise I won't do anything bad.'

Aki flung down his tools. 'Aw, come on then,' he groaned. 'Let's go.'

5

They put on their cloaks and fur hats and went out.
The weather had turned dry and cold. The thatched
roofs were gleaming with frost and the air was thick
with wood-smoke. It didn't take them long to walk
round the corner and down Troll Alley to the Staith.

'Hey, look!' said Dalla excitedly, as they rounded the
tall warehouse that stood on the corner. 'There's three
ships just come in.'

They pushed through the crowds to the quayside.
They had to dodge a group of boozy sailors and pirates
who were arguing loudly and shoving each other
around. They almost bumped into some giggling
floozy girls in exotic, low-cut dresses. A flea-bitten,
one-legged beggar came fawning around them, but
Aki chased him away. At last they were close enough
to see the ships properly.

Like all Viking ships, they were long and low, built of dark-tarred wood. Their decks were completely open and they had coloured sails. The first one was dripping with blood: it contained the headless body of a huge whale, which the sailors were busy slicing up. The next was a trading ship from somewhere far away and exotic. It was crammed with bales of silk, flagons of wine and sacks of sweet-scented spices. The third ship was crowded with passengers.

'Look at their funny clothes!' said Dalla.

'Foreigners,' said Aki. 'What a row they're making!'

Loud, agitated voices were drifting from the passenger ship. It was hard to catch what they were saying because of the foreign accents and dialects. But clearly, something rather odd was going on. Most of the passengers were huddled nervously together at the back. They seemed to be trying to keep out of the way of an enormous, dark figure standing on the side, poised to leap ashore.

'What's the matter with them?' said Dalla.

'Whoo!' cried Frodi pointing. 'Look at that!

Dalla did – and almost jumped out of her skin.

The dark figure on the side was a *bear!*

6

The bear gave a roar. Then it jumped down onto the quayside. Dalla scuttled behind Aki with a shriek. The bear heard her and lumbered round to face her... And they got another shock.

For it wasn't a bear after all. It was really a huge *man*! He was wearing a cloak made from a beautiful, shaggy brown bearskin. Its hood was actually the bear's head, with holes instead of eyes and gaping yellow fangs. It completely hid his face.

The man came striding down the quayside. The wind blew his cloak back, revealing a long, leather jerkin and heavy boots trimmed with grey wolf fur. Two huge swords dangled from either side of his belt.

'Oi! You crowd of feeble, dwarf-like wretches!' he roared. 'Come and help me! Take me to your king!'

Everyone on the Staith was staring at him, but

nobody answered or moved. Even the roughest men shrank back a little as he strode past.

'Why's he wearing a bearskin?' whispered Dalla.

'Do you reckon he's a berserk?' Frodi whispered back.

Aki nodded.

'Wow!' said Frodi under his breath. 'I've always wanted to see one!'

'What's a berserk?' said Dalla.

'Shh,' said Aki. His eyes were shining. 'They're warriors. But not ordinary ones, Dalla. They're supposed to be as strong as giants.'

'*Really?*'

'Ya. So strong that no one can hurt them!'

'And they have magic powers, don't they?' whispered Frodi.

'What do you mean?' cried Dalla.

'Shh,' Aki insisted. 'Ya, powers from *Odin*.'

Dalla shuddered. Odin All-Father was the most frightening of all the Viking gods. He only had one eye, but he saw and knew everything. He ruled over war, wisdom and magic. He was mysterious and terrifying.

'When berserks go into battle,' said Aki, 'Odin

whips them up and sends them completely crazy. They tear off their clothes...'

'And foam at the mouth,' said Frodi, 'and howl like wild beasts!'

'Ya,' said Aki, 'and they can make weapons blunt just by looking at them. They kill everyone in their path. And people say they can shape-change...'

'Turn themselves into animals!' cried Frodi.

'Ooh, that's scary!' Dalla squealed. 'But even so, I wish he'd do it now!'

'*Shh!*' hissed Frodi.

But the berserk had already heard her. He strode up to them.

'Hello Bear-Man,' said Dalla cheekily. 'My brothers here will help you.'

Frodi trod hard on her toe. Aki shook his head and drew in his breath. But it was too late.

For a long moment the berserk seemed to gaze at them all, though his eyes were hidden in the shadows of his great bear's-head hood.

Dalla turned bright red and bit her lip to stop herself giggling. Aki and Frodi stood their ground boldly.

'Ya, you boys will do,' said the berserk at last. He

wagged an enormous, hairy finger at them. 'Show me the way to the King's palace.'

Dalla grinned at her brothers, quivering with excitement.

'Of course, sir,' said Aki quickly. He nudged Frodi. 'It's this way.'

He waited for the berserk to fall in step with them. Then he led the way off the Staith.

7

The berserk strode by Aki's side. Frodi hurried after them. The drunks and floozies, beggars and sailors moved quickly out of their way. Dalla trailed behind. She caught Frodi's hand and tried to make him walk at her pace – but he slapped her off.

The berserk's legs were really long. For each step he took, the children – even Aki, who was quite tall – had to take two. There was a horrible, pungent smell about him, like rotting, maggoty meat. He kept grunting, clearing his throat and snorting as he walked.

They went up the steep rise of Marshy Street, then through several winding lanes lined with wooden houses. Soon they reached the palace square.

The King's palace was the most important building in the whole of Jorvik. None of the children had ever seen more than a tantalising glimpse of it, because it was surrounded on all sides by a high wooden fence. The only way into it was through a huge gate made of intricately twisted iron bars. This gate was always guarded, day and night, by two heavily armed soldiers.

The berserk motioned to the children to wait. Then he swaggered up to the guards.

At once the guards drew their swords. In a flash, the berserk reached inside his bearskin cloak and pulled out a massive sword of his own.

Aki and Frodi held their breath.

'I hope they're going to fight!' whispered Dalla.

But the berserk just gave a yelp of laughter. 'Save your strength, comrades,' he said. 'I'm not in the mood for spilling your guts out today. I want to see King Eirik Blood-Axe.'

'Can't,' said a guard with a thick brown beard and the coiled silver brooch of an officer. 'Haven't you heard? King Eirik's gone away with his pirate ships.'

'Has he now?' the berserk said softly. 'Just as I thought: he really is an old fool.' He laughed again, then said more loudly: 'Haven't *you* heard? A terrible danger is on its way to this town!'

Dalla gasped and clutched at her brothers. But the

guards just shrugged.

'Who's protecting the town in the king's absence?' the berserk demanded.

'Queen Gunnhild,' said Brown Beard.

'A *woman*?' guffawed the berserk. 'What a joke!'

'Many people fear Queen Gunnhild's power even more than the King's,' said Brown Beard quietly.

'Ha!' the berserk mocked him. 'The only power Queen Gunnhild has is that of a *witch*, isn't it? I've heard she's always lurking in dark rooms on her own, stirring up spells and potions. What use will that be when the enemy reaches town, eh?'

'Enemy?' said Brown Beard sceptically. 'I haven't heard of any foreign troops on the move.'

'No, it's not an army,' said the berserk. 'It's one man alone – a man who will bring such terror to this town that every child's life will be in danger. Go and tell your witch-queen about that, while she's dribbling over her brews. And tell her, she's lucky that a mighty warrior has come to save Jorvik – to do the job that her King has run away from!'

'Queen Gunnhild won't stand for talk like that,' Brown Beard warned him.

But the berserk just let out a roar like a wild beast,

then snapped his fingers suddenly at Aki and Frodi.

'It's time to move on, worms,' he said, 'take me to the market place.'

Aki nudged Frodi. Quickly they led the way down Meat Street and round the corner to the open space at the end.

'Here it is, sir,' said Aki.

The berserk nodded.

'Watch,' he said gruffly. 'Listen carefully. Then you will learn what I have come to Jorvik to do.'

8

The market place was very busy. Local farmers from miles around Jorvik had travelled in to set up tempting displays of meat, cheese, flour, vegetables and fruit. A musician was standing between the well and the fenced-in public bog hole, playing a jolly dance tune on his pipes. On the far side from him stood a little old English nun in a coarse black habit and headdress. She was humming along with the music as she unpacked a bag of sticky honeycombs onto a rickety table. Crowds of women, children and old folk carrying shopping baskets were milling around noisily.

The berserk strode into the centre. He grabbed a wooden crate from a nearby stall, hurled it down and leaped on top of it. Now his bear's-head towered above the crowd.

'Greetings, townspeople!' he roared.

The chatter died away. The music stopped. Everyone turned round to see what was going on.

'What are you all gawping at?' roared the berserk. 'You're afraid of me, aren't you? Well, don't worry, I've come to help you.'

No one answered.

The berserk gave a long, yodelling howl like a wolf: 'OW-OOH!' He drew one of his swords and swung it about his head.

'Let me show you what I'm made of!' he roared. 'Bring me a flaming log!'

Nobody moved. Some of the smaller children started to cry.

'What's he want a log for?' whispered Dalla.

The berserk whirled round at her voice and pointed at Frodi. 'You fetch me one, boy.'

Frodi hesitated.

'Better do what he says,' Aki urged him.

Frodi nodded and ran off. Very soon he was back, gingerly carrying a fat log he'd dragged from their own fire. One end was smouldering dangerously.

The berserk grabbed it from him and motioned Frodi out of the way. He dangled the log high above his head and fanned the end with his other hand.

Yellow flames began to leap from it.

Slowly, slowly, he lowered the flaming log towards the hideous, gaping bear's mouth. Suddenly he plunged the log underneath!

'UGGHH!' He gulped loudly.

The flames vanished.

'He's swallowed them!' someone shouted.

There was a sickening smell of singed fur.

People started clapping. Soon the market place was echoing with cheers and applause.

The berserk flung away the log and double-punched the air in triumph.

'That must be really dangerous,' whispered Dalla. 'Look at the horrible wounds he's got from it!'

The berserk's right arm was covered in ugly red burn scars and blisters. His left hand had a stump where one of his fingers was missing.

'Thank you, townspeople,' he said. 'Now you know that I am stronger than the elements, mightier than any man, beast or monster!'

A murmur of amazement ran round the marketplace.

'I suppose you're all wondering why I've come to Jorvik,' the berserk went on. 'Well, I've come to save you, townspeople – to save your *children*!'

'Save them from what?' called a market-woman from behind her wild nuts and berries stall.

'Your children are under threat from a terrible villain,' said the berserk. His voice was low and ominous. 'You must have all heard of that infamous brute, the terror of the North Lands – the evil child-killer Grim Gruesome?'

A ripple ran around the crowd. A few people gasped and tutted, but most just scoffed sceptically.

'Grim Gruesome?' called the musician, fiddling with his pipe. 'He's just a silly country bumpkins' tale, isn't he? A bogeyman to scare the little ones.'

'*Is* he, Aki?' squealed Dalla. 'Then why does Mam say, if I'm bad, I'll be snatched away by him?'

'Sshh!' hissed Frodi. 'Listen to the berserk.'

The berserk was making strange growling noises that echoed between the wooden buildings surrounding the square. 'You fools!' he said. 'You poor, ignorant fools! Grim Gruesome is as real as I am. And he is on his way here!'

'I always wondered if he *was* real,' whispered Frodi.

'Well, now you know,' said Aki. 'You see, Dalla, Mam was talking good sense when she warned you about him.'

Another ripple was spreading through the crowd.

'I've heard the stories about Grim Gruesome are definitely true,' said a tall woman with four small children in tow.

Several other mothers nodded earnestly:

'Ya, terrible things he did in the mountains of Norway!'

'...the way they say he tortured those poor children there...'

'I'll willingly trust this fellow if he can save the lives of our young ones...'

'Silence!' roared the berserk. 'Listen to my warning, all you women. Grim Gruesome has been spotted in this very kingdom. He is heading for this town! He has heard how Jorvik is overflowing with your innocent children. He's drooling at the thought of torturing them and gobbling them up. Any time now, he will arrive. And then, no child in this town will be safe.'

'Aw, but there's plenty enough guards and soldiers round the walls to keep him out!' an old man called. 'And they put chains across the river, you know, to stop enemy ships from getting in.'

'Don't fool yourself, Grandpa,' the berserk said. 'Grim Gruesome will swat them all down like flies. His horse can jump over the highest wall, squeeze through any barrier, swim the widest river. And he always works in disguise: those soldiers of yours won't even realise who he is until it's too late. How could King Eirik Blood-Axe abandon you all at such a terrible time?'

A woman screamed. Several small children started crying. Dalla clung on to Frodi's arm. Frodi and Aki stood very still, listening intently.

'Abandon us?' said a man selling vegetables, who had clearly travelled a long way in from the countryside. 'Why, where's the king gone?'

'He went off treasure raiding up in Scotland over two months ago,' said the musician disapprovingly. 'With three ships full of pirates.'

'Exactly!' roared the berserk, 'Your king has left your children to the mercy of a child-eating monster! Think about it, townspeople. Eirik Blood-Axe doesn't care about anything except filling up his already overflowing treasure chests with more silver. Do you realise who he's left in charge while he's away? His wife! A *woman*! A gibbering witch of a woman who spends all her time brewing up spells and potions! He doesn't have a clue how to rule his realm. He isn't a real king – he's a chicken! He deserves a scorn-pole. Hey, Grandpa! Lend me your stick.'

The berserk strode across to the old man and snatched his walking-stick from him. He thrust one end firmly into the muddy ground so that it stood upright. Then he grabbed a dead chicken from a meat stall and stuck it on top of the stick.

'There's your king!' he mocked. 'Not Eirik Blood-Axe· let's call him Eirik Chicken-Heart! Curse him, townspeople. Then come to me – because *I* can keep you all safe. *I* can save your children!'

The air was cold with shock. A few people laughed at the scorn-pole, and some actually cheered.

'But if Grim Gruesome *is* real – I've heard that no one can beat him,' said another woman loudly in a clipped accent. It was the English nun behind the honey stall.

At once the berserk rounded on her. 'What? Do you doubt me?' he roared. 'How dare you!'

The wrinkled old nun looked up at him calmly and shrugged.

The berserk gave a yelp of rage and spat at her from

under his hood.

'Grim Gruesome has never been tackled by a mighty warrior like me before,' he said. 'Have no fear, townspeople: I shall protect your city from this brute. I shall protect everyone – everyone who pays me.'

The nun shook her head with a sad smile and wiped his spittle carefully off her black dress. People began to whisper among themselves.

Another woman asked, 'But what about those that can't afford to pay?'

The berserk strode across to her. 'Give me a good weight of silver and I promise your whole family will be safe,' he said. 'But if you don't...' He shrugged. 'Well now, your poor children will just have to face Grim Gruesome all by themselves.'

9

'Here,' hissed Aki.

Quickly he led Frodi and Dalla out of the market place. They sneaked down an alley between two houses and stood under a spreading oak tree where no one could overhear them.

'We can't possibly pay him,' said Aki. 'The silver Pa left for us is only just enough to buy food. It might not even last us, if they're away for too long. If we give any to the berserk, we'll end up starving.'

'But we've *got* to pay him,' wailed Dalla, 'otherwise Grim Gruesome will get us. Can't we ask one of the neighbours for some more silver?'

'We can't go round begging,' said Aki. 'Mam and Pa would die of shame!'

'But we could just borrow...' pleaded Dalla

'No,' said Aki firmly. 'I don't need any help. I'm

quite capable of sorting this out myself. Now let me think...Pa always says it's best to tell the truth and be open with people. So maybe we should go and tell the berserk straight out that we can't afford to pay him at the moment, and why.'

'But berserks are supposed to have vicious tempers, aren't they?' said Frodi. 'I wouldn't like to get on the wrong side of him.'

'Don't be a namby-pamby,' said Aki scathingly. 'Why should he want to harm us, when he's come to Jorvik to protect everyone? Anyway, he ought to be feeling extra friendly towards us, considering we showed him the way to the market – *and* Frodi went and got that flaming log for him.'

'You're right,' said Frodi.

'So come on,' said Aki, 'let's get it over with. We'll be fine, so long as we're very careful what we say. And Dalla, just make sure *you* keep your mouth shut.'

She glared at him indignantly.

They went back to the marketplace. It was nearly midday by now. It had become very quiet. Most of the shoppers had gone. The stall-holders were packing up and setting off on their long treks home.

But the berserk was still there. Several women were

gathered around him. They were eagerly telling him their children's names and offering him silver bars and pennies. Aki waited until they'd all finished, then led the other two up to him.

'Excuse me, sir,' said Aki. 'We've got a bit of a problem. I'm afraid we can't afford to pay you at the moment. But we wondered if you could – please! – protect us anyway? We'll definitely pay you later.'

The berserk stood very still. They could feel his disapproval. 'Why can't you pay me?' he growled.

'Our parents are away,' said Aki guardedly. 'Only for a very short while,' he added quickly. 'They'll be back any time. But until they are, we haven't got enough...'

'Are you completely alone?' said the berserk.

Dalla was good at making people feel sorry for her. So she dabbed at her eyes with the corner of her apron and nodded earnestly.

'But you must have kinsfolk in town?' said the berserk.

Dalla shook her head sadly. She peered up at the berserk, trying to see under his bear's-head hood. But all she could make out was a dark, spiky beard and deep-set eyes flecked with blood.

'What?' said the berserk. 'No one to look out for you?'

'It's all right, we're fine,' said Aki quickly. 'Well, my brother and I are, anyway. But we're a bit bothered about our little sister Dalla here. She's always running off, you see, and getting herself into trouble. We're worried she might attract Grim Gruesome's attention.'

A farmer hurried by, carrying a crate of leeks on his shoulder. After him came the little old English nun, weighed down by her bag of unsold honeycombs – the last stallholder to leave. She smiled at Dalla as she went past.

The berserk turned his grotesque bear's-head hood and stooped down to peer at Dalla.

'What a fine girl,' he said. 'Just the sort of child that Grim Gruesome has a taste for. You're right. She could be in serious danger without my protection. I'll be happy to keep a special eye on her.'

'Oh, thank you, sir!' said Dalla proudly.

'But I can't protect her for nothing,' said the berserk to Aki. 'That would be unfair to all those who *have* paid me. Besides, as Odin All-Father said: *A gift always looks for a return.* So if you can't pay me, young man, you'll have to work for me instead.'

Aki didn't hesitate. 'Oh ya, I'll be honoured to do that, sir!' he said eagerly. 'I've always wanted to work for a great warrior like you. Especially to help you defeat a villain as evil as Grim Gruesome! What do you want me to do?'

'Come to me at first light tomorrow,' said the berserk.

'Right,' said Aki. 'Where will I find you?'

'You must all swear on Odin's name to tell no one else,' said the berserk. 'It would be disastrous if Grim Gruesome found out where I am staying.'

'Of course,' said Aki at once. 'I swear by Odin not to tell. Go on, Frodi.'

'I swear by Odin not to tell,' said Frodi.

'Go on Dalla,' said Aki.

'Odin's scary,' said Dalla. 'I'm not swearing on him.'

'SWEAR, GIRL!' the berserk snapped at her.

Dalla shook her head stubbornly.

'Actually, sir,' said Aki, 'she's such a scatterbrains, she'll never remember what you tell us anyway.'

'Indeed?' said the berserk. 'As you say, she certainly needs my protection.' He laughed in the back of his throat. Then he motioned to Dalla to move back until she was almost out of earshot.

'I'm staying at a secret place outside the town,' he told Aki in a low voice. 'You must leave through the South-West Gate and take the main road where the plough repairmen have their workshops. In due course, the road will fork. Ignore the branch that leads into the farmlands and take the forest way. Continue until you find a very large yew tree. You'll see a narrow deer-track leading off behind it. Go down that until you come to a ruined house at the end. Meet me there. Can you remember that?'

'Ya sir,' said Aki, 'but...'

'I will be waiting for you,' said the berserk. 'Make sure you're not late.'

Then he wrapped his bearskin cloak closer around him and strode away.

10

'Awf!' said Dalla. 'He stinks like a pig with diarrhoea when he gets close!'

'That's because he's too busy fighting great battles to bother with keeping clean,' said Aki.

He led the way out of the marketplace and round the corner towards home.

'I hope you don't come back from his house smelling like him,' said Dalla. 'I wonder what it's like there. I wonder if he's got any more of those bearskins... Oh Aki, I wish I could come with you and see it. Can I?'

'Don't be stupid!' snapped Aki. 'An important warrior like the berserk doesn't want an annoying little girl getting in his way – and nor do I.' He ran his fingers over the wisps of bum-fluff on his chin and drew himself up to his full height.

'But you promised Mam you'd look after me,' Dalla whined. 'She'll be furious when she finds out you've gone off and left me behind.'

'Mam's never furious with me,' said Aki smugly. 'Anyway, she'll be really pleased that I'm doing everything I can to get you under the berserk's protection, like all the other children. And you'll be perfectly safe, because Frodi will be looking after you, won't you, Frodi?'

'Farting giantesses!' cried Frodi. He scowled at Dalla. 'Don't expect *me* to keep her out of trouble. You know what she's like.'

'Stop making problems,' retorted Aki. 'Can't you see? This is an emergency! In Thor's name, just do what I say. And Dalla, you do everything that Frodi tells you – otherwise Grim Gruesome will come and pounce on you, before the berserk and I can destroy him!'

Dalla poked her tongue out at him.

'Watch out!' cried Frodi suddenly. 'There's a horse coming!'

A magnificent, dappled grey horse was cantering towards them down the street. They darted out of the way just in time. It wasn't an ordinary farm horse, but a beautifully groomed, long-legged thoroughbred, the type that nobles rode. Its bridle was splendid, with twisting silver decorations. The lady on its back was clearly very rich.

She was fair skinned with an elegant, arrogant face. Her thick, greying-blonde hair was swept up into elaborate coils and curls. Her flowing cloak was made of fine-spun purple cloth, trimmed with soft, white fur and fastened with a heavy gold brooch. More gold glittered on her fingers, her ears and her throat.

Two brawny men in red soldiers' tunics followed close behind her on brown horses.

'Ooh, look at her!' whispered Dalla.

To their surprise, the lady and her bodyguards stopped nearby.

'You there!' she called to the three children, 'come here.'

Aki led the way.

The lady leaned down from her horse. 'My guards saw you talking to that weird fellow in the bearskin, after everyone else had left the marketplace,' she said. Her voice was smooth, cultured – and angry. 'Do you know where he's gone?'

Aki and Frodi both shook their heads.

Dalla stared at the lady, open mouthed. Never in her life had she come so close to such splendid clothes, such dazzling jewellery. For a brief moment the lady held Dalla's gaze with her cold, pale grey eyes. Then she turned to the boys.

'You can have a piece of gold if you give me some useful information,' she said.

Dalla nudged Aki urgently. 'Gold!' she whispered. 'That's just what we need! Go on, all you've got to do is tell her what he said. Then you can pay the berserk and you won't have to…'

'*Shut up!*' Frodi whispered in her ear.

'I'm very sorry madam,' said Aki, 'but we swore on our honour by Odin not to pass on what the berserk told us. Our father would never forgive us if we broke an oath like that.'

Frodi nodded his agreement.

'Pah!' cried the lady. 'What do ignorant urchins like you know about honour?' She pulled angrily on the reins and turned her horse right round. 'The berserk is my enemy. I want him hounded out of the kingdom – or better still, killed!'

11

Everyone in the street had stopped to watch this encounter. As soon as the lady on the horse had disappeared, a girl of about Aki's age came running up to them.

'You lucky things!' she cried. 'However did you get to talk to her? What did she say? Was she scary?'

'She's beautiful, isn't she?' said Dalla. 'Did you see all that gold and the lovely fur on her cloak? She must be ever so rich.'

'Of course she's rich, goose face!' said the girl. 'Don't you realise who she is?'

Dalla looked at Aki. She looked at Frodi. They both shook their heads.

'You really are goose-brained, the lot of you!' cried the girl. 'That was Gunnhild Ozursdaughter – you know, the *Queen*!'

She ran off, chortling with laughter.

'Aw!' gasped Dalla.

'Thunderbolts! You refused to help Queen Gunnhild!' said Frodi. 'No wonder she was so furious!'

'I never realised,' said Aki. 'Well, thank the gods, we got away without telling her anything. And we managed to keep *you* quiet, Dalla. The last thing the berserk needs is her chasing after him when he's got such important work to do. Remember, he told us she's a witch.'

'Sorry,' said Dalla.

'I wondered why she was looking at you so strangely,' said Frodi. 'She was probably thinking of putting a spell on you.'

Dalla shuddered. 'Stop it!' she said. 'I'm scared enough about Grim Gruesome. Now you're making me worry about the Queen too!'

'It wouldn't surprise me if she's in league with Grim Gruesome,' said Frodi.

Aki nodded darkly. 'The berserk's our only hope of keeping you safe, Dalla,' he said. 'I'm really glad I'm going to help him. Because of that, he's bound to keep a special eye on you. Don't worry, whatever that witch of a Queen does, there's no way I'll give away the berserk's secret. Anyway, we've sworn not to on *Odin's* name. That's really serious. Imagine the dreadful things that would happen if we dared to break the oath!

12

The next morning Aki got up while it was still pitch dark. He put on his warm cloak and his fur hat and went out.

The streets were silent. A full moon and the frosty stars lit his way.

He hurried down to the bridge that crossed the River Ouse. Below it, lanterns were twinkling on the Staith as the day's first fishing boats came up from the sea. But beyond the bridge there was only darkness.

On the far side, he walked up Great Street. Every house there was shut up. The cooking fires hadn't started smoking yet. The town was empty apart from a few stray cats and dogs.

Soon he came to the South-West Gate. The watchman was half asleep and let Aki through without bothering to ask where he was going.

It was strange standing outside the town walls. Aki had only ever been out here a few times before. He walked quickly past the slumbering houses of Plough-Repairers Street and soon found himself in open countryside.

He followed the road on into the empty darkness. His heart was pounding with excitement as he imagined the adventure ahead.

13

Frodi and Dalla got up much later. Frodi stoked up the fire. They ate a big, lazy breakfast – and then realised they had no more food.

'We'd better go and buy some,' said Frodi.

He fetched a silver penny from the pot hidden behind the clothes chest and Dalla found a basket. Then they set out for the market.

It was busy there as usual. But the atmosphere was strangely subdued, quiet and very tense. There was no musician there today. All the younger children were clinging to their mothers. The adults were constantly glancing over their shoulders.

Dalla and Frodi traipsed round the various market stalls, arguing loudly. Frodi went to look at the round cheeses and slices of hard-dried meat. Dalla nagged him to buy some dark rye bread and pickled fish instead. As they couldn't agree what to get, they gave up looking at sensible food and went together to choose some honey from the English nun's stall.

A big crowd of older girls was already gathered round there. Some were holding out nuggets of silver for the nun's deliciously sticky honeycombs. Others were just chatting to her, and begging her to sing one of her funny English songs to chase away the horrors of Grim Gruesome. At last the girls wandered away, and Frodi got his turn to offer the nun half a silver penny.

'That one please.' He pointed to a really big piece.

The nun took his coin, wrapped up the honeycomb in a piece of clean linen and gave it to Dalla. As she worked, she struck up another song in her warbling, jolly voice.

'What are those peculiar words you're singing?' Dalla asked her.

'Well my dear,' said the nun, 'it's not just a song – it's a riddle too. Would you like me to translate it into your language?'

'A riddle?' said Dalla. 'What's that? Is it one of your funny English customs like going to church?'

'Shh!' Frodi hissed at her. 'You mustn't be rude.'

'Nonsense, nonsense,' beamed the nun. 'Your sister's just curious, and why not?' She turned to Dalla. 'It's a puzzle, my dear – a secret way of saying things.'

'Please,' said Dalla very politely, 'what does your riddle-song mean?'

The nun thought for a moment. Then she began to translate from English into Norse, reciting it very slowly in her curious, clipped accent:

'I crossed the ship's road from the east.
In silken robes I dance and feast.
With ring of cave-fire round my head
The noble pirate I have wed.'

'That *is* peculiar!' said Dalla. 'I still don't understand what it means.'

'Ah,' laughed the nun, touching her finger to her nose, 'that's for you to work out yourself, my dear. But I'll tell you this: the answer is a person.'

'Oh, who?' begged Dalla, jumping up and down.

'I'm not saying,' said the nun. 'But it's someone who might help you if you're ever in trouble.'

'Really? But why won't you tell me now?' said Dalla.

'It's more fun to work it out yourself,' said the nun mischievously. 'Besides, if I told you who it was, you wouldn't believe me.'

'Why not?'

'Thunderbolts, Dalla!' cried Frodi, 'can't you ever shut up?'

Dalla was about to thump him. But just then the air was rent by a terrible scream:

'Aaaghhh! Aaaghhh! Help!'

'Holy Father!' cried the nun. 'What's going on?'

A young woman carrying a toddler on her hip came running out of an alley. Her headscarf was all skew-whiff, her face was white and she was gasping for breath. The toddler was bawling.

'I've seen him!' the young woman gasped. She pointed back the way she'd come. 'Grim Gruesome! I'm sure it was him! I'm sure he was coming after me! A horrible, twisted man with bulging eyes! He was staring at my little Bodvar here!' She clutched the toddler to her bosom. 'Thor help us, what's happened to that berserk? Find him someone! We need him here now!'

At once the nun hobbled out from behind her stall, making comforting clucking noises. She helped the young woman and her toddler to sit down and gave the little one a wooden spoon dipped in runny honey to lick.

In the middle of all this fuss, two of King Eirik's soldiers came striding into the marketplace. They stood near the wicker fence of the public bog hole, talking quietly together and fingering their swords. Everyone looked at them expectantly.

'Didn't you hear?' a woman in a pink cloak yelled at them. 'This lady's seen Grim Gruesome! Get after him, you lazy toads! Or are you waiting for him to snatch someone's child away right under your noses!'

One of the soldiers stepped forward, holding up his sword to get the crowd's attention. It was Brown Beard, the guard the children had seen yesterday at the palace gate.

'Listen people!' he shouted. 'While King Eirik is away, Queen Gunnhild issues the following orders:

'One: You are not to be fooled by talk of Grim Gruesome. He's not real. He doesn't exist. He's just a country bumpkins' tale, a silly rumour put out to frighten people. The berserk is playing on your fears to stir up trouble and steal all your silver.'

People in the crowd shouted back angrily:

'Rubbish! That lady's *seen* him!'

'Our *children* are in danger!'

'What does Queen Gunnhild care? Her children are

all grown up anyway – and she's a witch!'

'You're meant to be protecting us!'

The other soldier twiddled his curly blond moustache. 'No we're not,' he said. 'Our job's to protect the Queen while King Eirik's away.'

'Pshaw!'

'What good's a king if he leaves his own subjects in danger?'

'Thanks be to Thor that the berserk's around!'

The soldiers exchanged words between themselves. Then Brown Beard called out:

'Order number two: The berserk has insulted the King and Queen. Therefore he is officially an enemy of Jorvik.'

'But he's come here to help us!' roared the crowd. 'He's on our side!'

'You'd better be careful,' Blond Moustache warned them. 'The Queen is set on revenge against the berserk. And you know she doesn't like people who try to oppose her.'

'Three!' shouted Brown Beard. 'Anyone who helps the berserk will be executed!'

'We're coming round to question everyone shortly,' said Blond Moustache. 'So if you have any information which will help us catch the berserk, make sure you speak up.'

Frodi squeezed Dalla's arm.

'Um, come on,' he said. 'I'll take you home.'

He began to steer her through the crowd, out of the market and back towards Cupmakers' Street.

'Leave off!' complained Dalla. 'I want to stay here and see what happens. Stop bossing me around, Frodi!'

Frodi shook her arm. 'Please, Dalla. You can't stay here, because if those soldiers ask us questions, you'll go and tell them exactly where the berserk is, won't you? Not only would that be breaking our oath...'

'I never swore it,' said Dalla.

Frodi sighed. 'Look Dalla, Aki's probably with the berserk right now – *with the King and Queen's arch-enemy.* Understand? Think what will happen to Aki if King Eirik's soldiers find them together!'

'Oh!' Dalla bit her lip.

They turned into Cupmakers' Street. Frodi hauled Dalla past the shop displays and into their little house.

'Just stay here Dalla,' he begged. 'You'll be much safer at home, with all these nasty goings-on.' He swallowed. 'I'm sorry if I've been horrible. I wish Aki hadn't gone off and left us. I'm trying my best to make sure you're all right. I promise I won't be long. You've got that piece of honeycomb in your basket to keep you going. And I'll buy some of that nice pickled fish you wanted.'

Before she could argue any more, Frodi slammed the door shut, locked it and clipped the key onto his belt.

Then he ran back to the marketplace muttering to himself, 'Thank Thor she's safely locked inside!'

14

By the time Frodi got back, the market was loud with excited gossip:

'If Grim Gruesome's here already...'

'Where's that berserk fellow? We paid him more than enough silver – why isn't he protecting us?'

'Maybe he's already chasing after Grim Gruesome.'

'What a cheek that hag of a Queen has, issuing all those orders. She doesn't care a flea's egg that our children are in deadly danger!'

'The berserk was right: she and King Eirik are a pair of useless chickens!'

'Lucky we've got the berserk to fight for us...'

Frodi made his way over to the pickled fish stall. He kept his eyes skinned, desperately hoping that the berserk would suddenly appear with Aki.

Surely they'll be back here any time now, he thought.

I wonder what Aki's got to do for him. Will he get involved in the actual fight with Grim Gruesome? He imagined his older brother covered in battle scars, and the whole town cheering him as a hero.

Just then he noticed that the two soldiers were jostling through the crowd. They were pulling people aside and firing them with questions.

Dwarf spit! thought Frodi. *What am I going to say if they question* me*? I'm not strong willed like Aki. I'm not sure how long I can hang on to the secret if they turn nasty.*

One of the soldiers glanced in his direction.

I should have stayed home with Dalla... But I've still got time to nip away!

Quickly he sidled into an alley. His mind was awhirl. *Supposing they've already spotted me? Better not go home now, in case they follow me...*

So at the bottom of the alley, he ran straight across King Street and onto the bridge that crossed the River Ouse. The wide grey water rushed beneath him. In the middle of the bridge he paused to catch his breath – and heard heavy footsteps pounding onto the wooden boards behind him. Glancing back he saw the blond-moustached soldier.

Frodi bolted to the opposite bank. *Don't give up!* he

thought. *Come on Frodi, you're one of the fastest lads in Jorvik. You can beat this brute!*

He turned left, pelted past the smart, new wooden houses of Shieldmakers' Street – and tripped over a big tabby cat that ran out straight in front of him. He stumbled, fell...leaped up again at once. But it was too late.

The soldier's hand landed heavily on his shoulder. 'Got you!' he barked. He yanked Frodi to a halt, forced him to turn round and grabbed his arms.

Close up, under his carefully twirled moustache, he wasn't much older than Aki. But he'd been trained to use an excruciating grip, and his blue eyes were hard and sneering.

'You've got something to hide, haven't you?' Blond Moustache said nastily. 'I know who you are: you're one of those lads seen talking to the berserk yesterday – on your own, when everyone else had scarpered – *whispering* with him, listening to his secrets. Queen's orders: tell me where he's hiding?'

Frodi clamped his lips shut and shook his head.

'Odin's eye-socket!' swore the soldier. He drew his sword from its scabbard. 'If you don't tell me, I'll slice off your ear.'

Frodi began to sweat. Blond Moustache twisted him round and moved his sword slowly towards the side of Frodi's head. Its blade was cold and sharp against his earlobe. Another tiny movement and it would pierce his skin.

I can't hold out! he thought desperately. *I'm a coward, I'm scared of being hurt! I can't help it – I'm going to betray the berserk and my own brother...!*

'STOP!' a deep voice roared. It came from behind Frodi.

The soldier's eyes widened. His sword-hand froze in mid-air. Frodi wriggled free, turned – and let out a gasp of surprise.

Behind them, right in the middle of the street, stood the berserk!

All down Shieldmakers' Street, doors creaked open. People surged out of their houses and crowded round, gawping, to see what the shouting was about.

'Come on then, help me!' Blond Moustache yelled at them, gesticulating wildly at the berserk. 'Don't you realise? This is the traitor that the Queen wants captured. Help me get him!'

There were plenty of men in the crowd. But not one of them moved.

The berserk reached into the shadows of his bearskin. He drew out one of his swords. It was a deadly looking, blood-stained weapon. He raised it – then fast as lightening, ran at Blond Moustache. Frodi yelped and leaped out of their way. The air rang with the clanging of metal.

The soldier was tough and quick. But the berserk was a hundred times stronger and faster. His eerie wolf-howls echoed on the wind down Shieldmakers' Street. He grabbed Blond Moustache, hurled him to his knees – then hacked at him with his blade until the muddy ground was awash with blood.

The young soldier groaned and whimpered. Then he keeled over.

'Eh, isn't the berserk strong!' a woman cried admiringly.

Everyone cheered.

'Good on you, bear-man!' another woman called. 'Now go and kill Grim Gruesome for us!'

The berserk stood, huge and awesome, panting like a wolf on heat. He rolled up his sleeves and rubbed his horrible, burn-scarred arm. He punched the air with his fist to acknowledge the cheers.

'Ya,' he roared, 'Grim Gruesome!'

Frodi couldn't take his eyes off the berserk. *He's saved me!* he thought. *Him, one of the mightiest warriors in the world, fighting for* me! He felt weak with relief and gratitude.

The berserk gripped the shaggy folds of his cloak with his heavily gloved hands.

Is he going to do that thing of tearing off his clothes? thought Frodi in wonderment.

But the berserk only pulled the bear's-head hood further forward and stashed his sword away.

Blood oozed from Blond Moustache's wounds.

'Frodi Snorrisson!' growled the berserk suddenly, turning to him.

'Y...ya, sir,' answered Frodi. His heart was pounding.

'I was looking for you,' said the berserk. 'Where have you been? Come with me.'

Frodi was in a daze, a wonderful dream. *Now he wants me to help him!* he thought. *My hero!*

But then, with a sinking feeling, he remembered Dalla.

'I...oh no, sir, I'm afraid I can't,' said Frodi. 'You see my little sister...I can't leave her.'

'Nonsense!' roared the berserk. 'Hurry!'

A great man like this, thought Frodi. *I can't refuse him!* Guiltily, he took a step towards the berserk. He glowed as he felt the crowd's astonished eyes on him.

The berserk nodded his bear's head then led the way briskly round the corner and up Great Street. Frodi followed him in a daze.

15

You might think that Dalla was feeling scared and lonely, locked up on her own in the little, one-roomed house in Cupmakers' Street – but not a bit of it.

She took the honeycomb out of her basket and ate a big hunk of it. Then she thought: *Aha! Snotty-nosed Frodi has forgotten: there's a spare key hidden underneath the flour jar.*

The jar stood in the corner next to the weaving loom. It didn't take her long to tip it up and prise out the key.

Goose poo to you, Frodi! she thought. *You can't make me stay at home after all!*

She unlocked the door and slipped out, clipping the key onto her belt.

Ya! I can go where I want. There's no one to stop me!

She waved to the man next door, who was busy

serving a woman with five noisy children at his shoe repair stall. Then she ran down Troll Alley to the Staith to see if any new ships had come in.

They hadn't, so next she went up to the palace to see if anything interesting was going on there. It wasn't, but Dalla didn't mind. She loved just wandering around town.

I'd better keep well away from the marketplace, she thought.

So she strolled over the bridge across the river, along Great Street and back again. She explored all the shops that lined many of the narrow streets. She peered into the quiet, dark churches where the English people worshipped their strange God. She gazed up and down the river. She begged scraps of food from friendly passers-by: what she couldn't eat at once, she crammed into her purse. She stroked lots of cats. She listened avidly to all the town gossip.

Most of this gossip was about Grim Gruesome. You should have heard it! There was no more talk of him being a harmless tale. Instead, people said he was a real, live, evil brute who pulled his victims apart limb by limb and swallowed children alive! It made Dalla's flesh creep... But she couldn't resist pricking up her ears just the same.

She kept on wandering and eavesdropping for the rest of the day. When she got home, dusk was falling.

Uh-oh, she thought: *Frodi's bound to be back by now. He's going to be mad at me for sneaking off after he told me to stay here.*

But to her surprise, Frodi wasn't there.

Maybe he's out looking for me, she thought. And – unusually for Dalla – she felt just a little bit guilty.

The fire had burned right down to a few glowing embers. She put some more logs on it, and beat them with the poker until the flames flared up again to warm the room.

I wonder how long he'll be, she thought.

She sat on the wall-bench next to the door and listened. She heard footsteps passing, and the woman who lived across the street yelling at her son. She heard a pack of stray dogs running past, barking and yelping. But Frodi didn't come.

Never mind the guilt: now she started to feel nervous. It was so quiet in the house. She'd never had to look after herself before. *But home's the safest place to be,* she thought. She got up and locked the door like Frodi had done.

She was too exhausted from her long day of walking to get herself into a state. So she lay down on the bench, pulled some blankets over herself, curled up – and fell fast asleep.

Dalla didn't wake up until the next morning.

The house was cold because the fire had gone out. It was dark because most of the lamps had run out of oil. She was hungry and thirsty.

And there was still no sign of Frodi.

Wherever can he be? she thought. *He only popped back to market to buy a few things. Even if he went to look for me, why hasn't he come home?*

She chewed her fingers. *Aki said he had to look after me! Frodi always does what Aki says. So something must have happened to him – something bad!*

Her heart missed a beat. *Oh no! What if the soldiers took him away to the Queen and she's going to execute him for keeping the berserk's secret?*

Then, even worse, all the dreadful gossip she'd heard about Grim Gruesome came crowding back into her head. *Supposing Grim Gruesome's snatched him away?*

Dalla felt sick. She slid off the wall-bench, unlocked the door and dashed out to use the bog hole in the yard. Then she came back in and went to fetch a drink from the beer pot. But they hadn't thought of buying any more beer yesterday, and it was empty.

It's not fair! she thought. *Just when I'm really thirsty. Aw, I'll have to go out to the well and drink some of that horrible water instead.*

She smoothed her clothes, combed her hair and put on her cloak. She fetched a wooden cup from the shelf and went outside again, locking the door behind her.

It was still only half-light.

The nearest public well was round the corner, in King Street. The whole street was deserted as she ran along it. When she reached the well, she hauled up a bucket and filled her cup from it with murky water. She stood close to the low, wicker fence to drink, huddled against the dawn chill in her cloak.

Oh, oh, oh, she thought, *whatever shall I do?* She still felt sick. Her stomach had tied itself into a knot of fear.

If only there was someone to ask! But all the neighbouring families had already drawn their morning water. Now everyone else was safe indoors, gathered round their fires, eating breakfast. Tantalising smells of cooking smoke and barley-porridge drifted out through the thatched roofs and along the street towards her.

I wish I knew how to get the fire started again, thought Dalla. *I wish Mam and Pa hadn't gone away. I wish Aki and Frodi were still here...Oh, farting giantesses! I wish I hadn't spoken to the berserk when we first saw him down the Staith. Then he wouldn't have known who we were, and Aki wouldn't have gone off with him – and I wouldn't be left here all on my own! Goddess Freyja help me! It's all my fault!*

Bravely she wiped away the tears. *I suppose I could knock on one of the neighbours' doors and ask for help...But I can't disturb them so early.*

At the far end of the street, suddenly a figure appeared out of the twilight. It came sauntering along towards her. Even from the distance she could see it was someone massively tall and broad. Slowly it came closer.

Dalla made out the bearskin cloak and hood of the berserk.

Thank the gods! she thought. *He's come back. Surely Aki can't be far behind him?* Her spirits lifted.

'Sir!' she called, 'SIR!' And she began to run towards him.

16

The berserk stopped and waited for her.

'Dalla Snorrisdaughter,' he said softly as she reached him.

'Where's Aki?' cried Dalla.

The berserk didn't answer.

She looked up the street, but there was no sign of her elder brother. She took a step back and peered up at the berserk. His beard poked out, dark and coarse from under the brown bear's-head. In its shadow, she could just make out the glinting of his eyes. His stink of rotting meat was so foul, it made her retch.

The early morning was very still.

At last the berserk spoke. 'I've come to tell you that both your brothers are at my hideout, Dalla.'

'*Both* of them?' cried Dalla. 'Frodi as well? I never realised… But is he all right? He never said…'

The berserk gave a snort of a laugh.

'Oh please, sir,' said Dalla, 'as they're both helping you now, can I come too? I'm very...'

'No, Dalla. Don't try and persuade me to put you in danger,' the berserk answered.

'But it's not fair to leave me out!' she cried. 'Anyway, my brothers aren't supposed to leave me on my own. They promised Mam and Pa they wouldn't! Supposing Grim Gruesome catches me while they're away?'

The berserk held out his hand. His huge gloves were made of shaggy black fur, darker and softer than the bearskin.

'Trust me,' he said. He gave a growl of a laugh. 'You know I am the only one who can save you from Grim Gruesome.'

He caught her hand. His grip was firm. The fur was soft and warm against her skin. Dalla felt strangely light headed.

'Go home,' he said softly.

Before she could argue any more, the berserk dropped her hand and turned his back on her. He strode briskly away towards the river.

For a few moments Dalla just gazed after him in

despair.

But then she thought, *Why should I do what he says? Why should Aki and Frodi have all the adventures and leave me out? They know how badly I want to see the berserk's hideout. The pigs! They could easily have asked him to include me. Well, I'll follow him anyway, that's what I'll do!*

It was completely light by now. For another moment she hesitated. Then she hitched up her dress and ran after him.

17

By the time Dalla reached the riverbank, the berserk was already on the far side of the bridge. She could see his bear's-head hood bobbing up and down as he strode quickly up Great Street. Then a horse-drawn wagon came clattering up behind her, and she had to stand and wait until it had passed. By the time she stepped onto the wooden slats of the bridge, the berserk had disappeared from view.

She ran after him.

But has he gone straight up Great Street, she wondered, *or turned off down one of those alleys?*

Dalla normally just followed her nose and went where she fancied. She wasn't used to working things out. She stopped for a moment.

If only I could remember what the berserk told Aki and Frodi about how to get to his house. Hold on, wasn't it something about a gate? Ya, I'm sure it was: the South-West Gate – and that's just up here, at the end of Great Street! Lucky I know my way around town.

Dalla walked quickly on and soon came to the town wall and the heavy iron gate.

'Woah there, lass,' said the watchman, stepping out of the arch as she approached. 'Where do you think you're going?'

'Out there. I've got to find my older brothers,' said Dalla, pointing through the gate.

'What? On your own? Certainly not!' said the watchman. 'I don't care what Queen Gunnhild says, I reckon Grim Gruesome is a real live thug. I'd never forgive myself if I let you go out there and then he caught you.' He peered more closely at her. 'Hey, you're Dalla Snorrisdaughter, aren't you? You little scamp, running wild at this time of the morning! And I bet you never gave your mam that rune-stick!'

'I did!' said Dalla indignantly. 'Anyway, I saw that berserk go through the gate just now. So if Grim Gruesome *did* come along, the berserk could save me!'

'You're right, the berserk did just pass through here,' said the watchman. 'But a great warrior like him doesn't want a silly little girl holding him up. Now hop it!'

81

He wouldn't listen to her pleading. Dalla sighed and turned away. There was a patch of wasteland to the left of the gate. She stomped onto it gloomily and kicked her way through piles of dead leaves. Soon she found herself standing in the middle of a copse of ancient trees.

She stared through them and up at the town wall.

Actually, it's not that high, she thought.

Then she noticed a huge beech tree right next to the wall. Some of its branches hung over onto the other side.

Dalla was out of sight of the watchman. The copse hid her from any passers-by in the street. There was nothing to stop her.

She lifted up her dress and apron and tucked the hems into her belt. Then she stood under the lowest branch of the tree – leaped up – and managed to catch hold of it.

She hauled herself onto the branch, then clambered up to the next one. And the next. Now she was level with the top of the wall. She turned awkwardly – made a sort of leap – and ended up sitting lopsidedly on top of the wall itself.

It looked a long way down to the other side. She

was too scared to jump. But she turned round gingerly and came down backwards, grabbing at jutting-out stones, sticking her feet into holes. At last she reached the ground. She was outside Jorvik for the first time in her life!

'Phew!'

She pulled her dress and apron back into place and gazed around. Luckily she had landed in a deserted alley. No one had seen her.

At the end of the alley she found the road. It was lined with noisy workshops, and the men there were much too busy to notice her. She turned onto it and began to walk away from the walls.

Soon she was in open countryside. The beaten mud road stretched on and on ahead of her. It was edged by low stone fences and, beyond them, fields of crops and cattle.

This looks like the road the berserk told Aki to walk along, she thought. *But where does it go? And whatever will I find at the end of it?*

18

Dalla passed a small oak wood where a lot of pink-and-black pigs were snuffling in the mud, then a big farmhouse surrounded by huts and a smithy. In the distance, groups of slaves were working in the fields. But she didn't see anyone close enough to talk to.

Being a town girl, Dalla wasn't used to walking such a long way. Her feet soon grew sore and her legs ached.

After a long time, she came to a fork in the road. One branch continued onwards through open farmland. The other led into a spreading forest.

Now which way? she wondered.

And almost at once, the berserk's voice came echoing into her head: '*...take the forest way...large yew tree...deer track leading off behind it...ruined house at the end...*'

'So there, Aki!' she said out loud, 'I *can* remember things!'

She peered into the forest. All she could see were brambles and darkness.

Thor's thunderbolts! She thought. *That must be the way, but Mam says forests are full of wolves and robbers!*

She sank down on the side of the road and groaned.

'Ooh, my poor feet! I'll have to have a rest while I think what to do.'

She pulled off her shoes. The soles were torn to shreds. Wretchedly, she hurled them into the trees.

She was desperately hungry.

Hold on, she thought, *there's those scraps of food people gave me yesterday when I was walking round town... I'm sure I put the bits I couldn't eat into my purse.*

She opened the leather pouch that dangled from her belt and tipped it out into her lap. Sure enough, there were three broken oat biscuits, several strips of hard bacon and a small crab apple. She munched on them greedily.

Just as she was gulping the last mouthful of biscuit crumbs, she suddenly heard a noise. Horse's hooves! They were coming towards her through the forest. She jumped up hopefully.

Maybe that's a farmer coming and he'll tell me if it's safe to go in there, she thought. *Oh – but supposing it's a robber...!*

The horse burst out from the forest. It didn't have a rider of any kind. It didn't even have a bridle. It came cantering wildly towards her.

It was beautifully groomed, sleek and proud. In fact, it was a beautiful creature in every way.

It was bigger even than Queen Gunnhild's horse, and pure, glossy black. Its mane and tail were both very thick, pale grey: they seemed to shimmer like silver.

As soon as the horse saw Dalla, it stopped dead and gazed at her from huge, black eyes.

Dalla jumped to her feet.

The horse neighed and tossed its head at her. It seemed friendly, so Dalla went cautiously up to it. She held out the apple core.

The horse stood very still. It took the core from her gently and crunched it up. It nuzzled her fingers.

'Oh, you beautiful thing!' cried Dalla. 'If only you could help me! Is this the way to the berserk's house? Is it safe to go into the forest?'

The horse neighed again, tossing its head. Then it

began to walk slowly back the way it had come. After a few paces it stopped and turned to look at her.

'You're telling me to follow you, aren't you?' said Dalla. 'I'm sure you are. Well, if I'm going to find Aki and Frodi, I suppose I'll have to risk it.'

So she swallowed her exhaustion. With bare feet, she ran after the horse into the trees.

19

The road through the trees was flat but narrow and very winding. It was overhung with branches and tangled thorns, and littered with leaf mould. The horse broke into a canter. Soon it was so far ahead that Dalla lost sight of it completely.

She stopped. The forest seemed to stretch on and on in all directions: tree behind tree behind tree. She began to panic. She nearly turned back...

But in the distance, she suddenly saw the dark, spreading mass of an enormous yew tree. *That must be the one the berserk said about,* she thought.

She gritted her teeth and trudged on.

Soon she found herself directly in front of the yew, gazing up at its canopy of dark green needles.

Didn't he say there was a deer track leading off behind it? Dalla peered round the broad, scaly trunk. *Ya, there is!*

She squeezed past the yew and started down the well-worn track. It was narrow and very overgrown, but clear enough to follow. A short way along it she reached a clearing. In the middle of this stood a half-ruined house.

The broken end of the house was a mess of fallen stones and rotting wood. But the other end was still soundly thatched and in good condition. Its door was tightly shut.

There was no one around. But strange, muffled noises drifted from behind the house.

Dalla's heart was racing. She crept up to the door. She put up her fist and knocked on it.

Nothing happened. Nobody came.

There was no handle or latch. She pushed. The door was locked.

But now she could hear someone shouting behind the house – someone in a furious rage!

Dalla pressed herself against the front wall. She crept along it to the end. Then she peered cautiously around it.

20

She saw a yard, divided by rough wooden fences into pens. All the pens were empty except for one, which contained a bedraggled sheep. It was stamping, pushing against the fence and butting it hard with its horns.

'Maaah!' it bleated. 'Maaaah!'

A mess of black, pea-like droppings fell steaming from its backside.

Standing to one side of the sheep-pen was the berserk.

He seemed even taller than Dalla had remembered. The fangs of his bear's-head hood seemed sharper and yellower. And behind him stood Frodi!

Dalla's heart turned over. *What's the matter with him?* she thought.

For Frodi looked as pale as death; and he was

quaking like a leaf.

'...what have you done to my brother?' came Frodi's voice. But was it really him?

Why is he squeaking? thought Dalla. Her heart was beating so hard, she could scarcely breathe.

'Oh, he's still alive,' the berserk said. 'He's right here.'

Dalla could see that Frodi's whole body was rigid. She heard his weird, high-pitched voice again: 'What...what do you mean?'

'Turn round Frodi,' said the berserk.

He was pointing towards the sheep pen. Frodi turned as he was ordered and looked frantically all round it. There was no sign of Aki.

'I can't see him! Where is he?'

'There,' said the berserk.

'But there's no one there. There's only the sheep.'

'Maaaah!' bleated the sheep. *'MAAAAH!'* It jerked its head up. It stared at Frodi from sickly yellow eyes with long, slit-like pupils.

The berserk said, 'The sheep is Aki. Aki is the sheep.'

'I...I don't know what you're talking about!' Frodi cried.

Cold sweat dripped down Dalla's neck and shoulders.

'You must realise, Frodi,' said the berserk, 'that to become such a mighty warrior, I have had to master all the darkest skills of Odin – including shape-shifting.'

Frodi let out a strangled cry.

Dalla flattened herself even closer to the wall, terrified lest the berserk should spot her. She bit her tongue to stop herself from screaming.

The berserk said: 'I can transform myself into a wild beast. And I can transform others, too.'

He took a step towards Frodi. Frodi tried to back away, but he crashed into the sheep-pen. Behind him the sheep was still butting its fence and crying out pitifully.

'Turn round, take a good look at him, Frodi,' said the berserk. 'Doesn't he look and sound exactly like the real thing?'

'Wh...what?' Frodi reached back and gripped the fence with a trembling hand.

The berserk gave a bellowing laugh. 'Last night,' he hissed, 'I drank a whole jar of steaming wolf's blood. It turned me mad, Frodi. It filled me with enough dark power to change your brother.'

He paused. A breath of wind sighed through the forest, then died.

'Tonight,' said the berserk, 'I will drink more and do it again. And when the frenzy comes upon me this time, I shall transform myself into a bear – a *real* bear, Frodi, not just this dead beast's skin. And when that is done, I shall transform YOU!

'Bit by bit. You'll find a patch of skin sprouting scrappy fur. Horns leaching up from the hollows of your brain. A tail oozing like a worm from your backside. You will be unable to stand upright. The change will creep over you like an evil rash, itching and aching, tormenting you. You'll get the squirts and faint with horror... And when you wake in the chill of dawn you'll have turned into a pathetic, bleating goat.

'A sheep and a goat, Frodi. Your brother and you. Then I, the ravenous bear, will tear you both apart, limb by limb – like this!'

Suddenly, with startling strength he grabbed the sheep by its horns, lifted it from the ground and spun it round through the air. When he dropped it, the sheep staggered and groaned. It fell awkwardly to its knees, half-stunned.

Dalla felt bile rising in her throat. The berserk continued:

'But even after I've eaten you both, Frodi, my hunger still won't be satisfied. For I crave a taste of your pretty little sister too. She will be the juiciest morsel of all. Oh, I gave her a chance: I did try to lose her.' He gave a snort of laughter. 'But she is like every wretched child: a helpless moth drawn to my flame. Ya, I have a delicious feeling in my innards that she is on her way to me now, creeping closer and closer, even as we talk. Ya, Frodi, I will have her too.'

'You can't!' Frodi spluttered.

'I can. I will. Look at me boy!'

21

Slowly, very slowly, the berserk flung back the bearskin cloak. It hung loosely over his shoulders like a peeled, raw skin. He pushed back the bear's-head. He unclipped the silver, snarling-wolf brooch that held the whole thing in place. The bearskin slithered off him to the ground.

Dalla was trembling so much she could hardly hide herself.

Underneath, the berserk was wearing another, more ordinary cloak and hood. It was the colour of midnight, and the hood was pulled right forward. Dalla still couldn't see his face.

The berserk swept the front of this cloak out of the way. He rolled up the sleeves of his tunic, showing off his one arm almost as hairy as the bearskin, and the other a smooth, red mess of weeping burn-sores and scabs.

He held up his huge fists then slowly opened them. Dalla saw him move them towards Frodi's face, clawing at the air. There was the hairy hand with the missing finger: in its place was an ugly stump, covered in black scabs and crusted pus.

Dalla's head was swimming. The darkness of the forest rushed in on her.

'You?' she heard Frodi say, choking and spluttering as he tried to get the words out, 'you look like... You're not...?'

The berserk pushed him easily to the ground.

'Ya,' he said softly. 'The story I spun in the market place was all lies. How easily I tricked almost every man, woman and child in the town! But none has given me so much fun as you three pathetically eager brats. What? Surely you didn't really expect me to protect you? How eagerly you all plunged into the trap I set for you! As for your cocky older brother here: the fool actually wanted to *help* me! Ah-ha-ha!'

His coarse laugh boomed and echoed round the stillness of the forest clearing.

'Didn't any of you guess what I was up to? Did none of you realise?

'*I* am Grim Gruesome!'

22

Dalla fled. Her heart and stomach were a sickly, churning mess. Her legs shook so much, she could hardly stay upright.

The trees seemed to crowd in on her, full of strange cracklings and gusts of wind. But somehow she staggered and stumbled back along the deer-track to the road. She ran along it until she had no more strength left. Then, shakily, she sank down onto the verge.

The autumn sun was low in the sky, glowing on the distant farmhouses. How ordinary they looked, after the horrors of the forest!

'Whatever shall I do?' she sobbed.

Confused thoughts and grotesque pictures wove in and out of her head:

I can't manage without Aki and Frodi. Oh Thor! Grim

Gruesome's going to kill them! Mam and Pa will say it's my fault! They'll whip me, I know they will! Thunderbolts! That's if Grim Gruesome doesn't kill me first. Oh, oh, oh!

She was so tired that she lay down in the grass.

Maybe I should just wait here, she thought, *and die of cold or starvation. Better than being eaten alive by Grim Gruesome!*

The sun set. In the dusk it grew chilly and the grass glistened with dew. Dalla drifted into an exhausted, restless sleep.

As she tossed and turned, a horse and wagon came down the road and stopped. A ruddy faced man jumped down from it and stared down at her:

'Are you all right, lass?' he said loudly.

Dalla jerked awake at his voice.

'No, NO!' she screamed.

She sat up and blinked at the wagoner. When she was sure he wasn't Grim Gruesome, she said,

'Please help me! Can you take me back to Jorvik?'

'Of course I can,' said the wagoner. He sounded normal and friendly. The edges of Dalla's fear began to melt away. 'Come on then, jump in.'

He helped her into the wooden wagon. She squashed herself on the floor between a sack of barley and a pile of carrots. The wagoner climbed up in front of her and jerked the reins until his horse resumed its slow plodding along the road. He looked at her curiously.

'So what are you doing out here all by yourself, lassie?'

Dalla said in a wobbly voice: 'I...I was running away.' She swallowed. 'I've seen Grim Gruesome! He's caught my brothers!'

The wagoner gave a kindly laugh. 'Grim Gruesome? Eh, you've got a strong imagination! You're as bad as my wife. Ever since she heard about that villain, she's been begging me not to go out of town – reckons as soon as I'm gone, he'll be sneaking in to snatch away our little ones.'

'But I'm not imagining it!' cried Dalla. 'This is real! I tell you, I've actually *seen* Grim Gruesome. You've got to believe me!'

The wagoner drew in his breath and drove on in silence for a few moments. At last he said: 'Well...you've certainly got yourself frazzled up about something. But Grim Gruesome...!' He shook his head. 'It can't possibly be... Did you say he got hold of your brothers?'

'Ya,' said Dalla wretchedly.

'Well, true or false, there's nothing *I* can do,' the wagoner said quickly. 'I'm no fighting man. Best thing is, soon as you're home, get your pa to find out where that berserk fellow's got to. He's the one to sort things out: he'll probably be straight out to rescue them.'

'But my pa's away,' said Dalla, trying to keep her voice steady. 'And anyway, the berserk… Oh, I know this sounds impossible, but the berserk *is* Grim Gruesome! They're exactly the same person. That bearskin he wears – it's just a disguise!'

'Now, now,' the wagoner interrupted her, 'you're getting all muddled up and into a tizzy, aren't you – and that's not going to help things. I tell you what, I'm very good at calming folk down. My youngest lad, he's got a temper like a mad dog, but I can always make him laugh. Listen: I'll tell you his favourite joke. See, there was…'

'I'm not in the mood for jokes,' Dalla interrupted him. 'I'm trying to tell you, the berserk isn't…'

'A riddle then!' cried the wagoner. 'You're right, jokes are useless when you're worried silly. But you know those English riddles that are going round? They force you to think hard, so they take your mind off other, nasty things. Try this one.'

He began to chant in a childish, sing-song voice:

'From woman's belt or brooch I swing

I am a very magic thing

I fit a hole, though stiff and stout

You'll hear me click to turn about.

What am I?'

Dalla bit her lip and shook her head.

'It's a key!' cried the wagoner triumphantly. 'Here, have some bread and cheese. My wife gave me more than I could eat this morning.'

Dalla took what he offered and crammed it hungrily into her mouth.

'Here's an easier one,' said the wagoner as she chewed it.

'Shining like ornaments in a high lord's home

I am water turned to bone.'

'Is it silver?' said Dalla wearily.

'Wrong!' chuckled the wagoner. 'The answer's ice. See, when water freezes it's as hard as bone, and ...'

The wagoner was right. His silly banter really did lift Dalla out of the depths of horror. As she began to breathe more easily, suddenly she remembered the strange rhyme that the English nun had told her.

'Oh sir,' she cried, 'as you're so good at solving riddles, can you tell me what this one means? I've probably got it all jumbled up, but it was something like this:

'I crossed the ship's road from the east.

*In silken robes...*um...*dance and feast.*

Something about a... *a ring – round my head*?

And *cave-fire* – but whatever's that? Then:

*The noble...*er...*noble pirate...*

Oh, ya, it has to rhyme, doesn't it?

...cave fire round my head,

the noble pirate I have wed.'

The wagoner asked her to say it again. Then he had a long think.

Dalla waited, biting her nails. The horse plodded steadily along. The wagon creaked. It was completely dark by now and growing very cold. Her fingers and bare toes felt like ice.

'Got it!' the wagoner said suddenly. *'In silken robes, dance and feast* – it's someone rich, sounds like a woman. *Cave fire* is a poet's words for gold. So she's wearing a gold band round her head – that must be a crown. And wed to the *noble pirate* – well, everyone knows King Eirik Blood-Axe isn't just our chief nobleman – he also goes treasure raiding like a common pirate. And he ruled Norway before he came here, so he and his wife crossed the *ship's road* – the sea – from the east. There's only one possible answer: it must be Queen Gunnhild! Eh, that's a real clever one, that is.'

Dalla's head was spinning.

Queen Gunnhild! she thought. *The nun said the answer would help me – but I can't ask the* Queen *for help. She's supposed to be a dangerous witch!*

She snatched at a straggly strand of her hair and twisted it round and round her fingers.

Oh, but it was the berserk – Grim Gruesome! – who said that. And he's *a liar and a trickster. So if he makes out the Queen's wicked, she's probably really* good!

Her head was aching like mad. But she forced herself to keep thinking.

All right, just supposing the Queen is good: would she help me? Of course not! She doesn't even believe Grim Gruesome's real. She'd laugh at me.

Dalla gazed hopelessly into the darkness. The shadow of the town walls loomed ahead in the distance.

Or...would she? After all, she hates the berserk too,

because he insulted her and King Eirik. Even if she doesn't believe that the berserk is really Grim Gruesome, she's desperate to know where he's hiding. And I can tell her! If I do, she might send her soldiers out to kill him. Oh Ya!

She looked at the wagoner, but he was whistling to himself and she didn't like to trouble him any more.

I wish I could ask Aki's advice. But he's not here, is he? Huh! He always makes out he's so clever, but he couldn't save himself from being tricked, and turned into a stupid sheep! Goose poo to you, Aki! I'll never look up to you again!

She sighed.

Trying to get Queen Gunnhild to help has to be better than just hiding and waiting for Grim Gruesome to pounce on me too, she thought. *Ya. I think I'll have to risk it.*

23

The wagoner drove Dalla through the South-West Gate and all the way up Great Street. He dropped her off just by the river. It was dark by now, but there was almost a full moon. She crossed the bridge. This side of town was still quite busy with women and children hurrying home and men going out drinking. Many of them carried smoking oil lamps to light the way through the narrow lanes.

Frost was gathering on the thatched roofs. Without shoes, Dalla's feet were freezing and her legs felt strained and wobbly. Even so, she managed to run most of the way to the palace. A dog growled threateningly at her, but nothing could frighten her after Grim Gruesome. She passed a house with the door ajar and stopped to drink in the comfort of its yellow lamplight. She hurried quickly past a man and woman standing in the shadows shouting drunkenly and slapping each other.

Soon she reached the palace square. It was lit by flaming torches in a row of iron holders along the top of the palace fence. Brown Beard and another soldier stood guarding the gate.

Dalla stopped a short way off. She took the comb from her belt and dragged it through her tousled red hair. She smoothed down her torn dress and cloak. She fixed her face into a polite smile. She cleared her throat.

Then she went up to the soldiers and said, 'Please can you take me to the Queen? She wants to know where that berserk is hiding, doesn't she? Well, I can tell her.'

The soldiers looked at her suspiciously.

'You've got a cheek, Tatty Cloak!' sneered Brown Beard. 'How could *you* know something like that? Besides, the Queen doesn't see beggars.'

'But it's vital information!' cried Dalla desperately. She clenched her fists. 'She needs to know it. I'm not going away until I see her – I'm not!'

Brown Beard rolled his eyes and tried to grab her but she darted out of reach.

'Anyway, the Queen knows who I am!' said Dalla. 'She stopped me and my brothers outside the marketplace the other day because she'd heard we'd been talking to the berserk. My brothers wouldn't tell her anything because the berserk made them swear not to – but *I* never swore. And I know...'

The two guards looked at each other.

'I remember seeing the brothers,' said Brown Beard in a low voice. 'They were grovelling round the berserk like slaves.'

'Wasn't one of them the lad that young Svein was chasing yesterday?' said the other guard. 'You know, when the berserk suddenly appeared out of the blue and slaughtered him?'

'Ya, that's right,' said Brown Beard. 'If this is really the sister...' he lowered his voice, but Dalla could still hear him. '...I've heard people say she's a minx. Well, you can see she's a bit...'

'So what? If she can give any genuine information, the Queen'll want to hear it.'

They both stared hard at Dalla.

'Aw...come on then,' said Brown Beard. He beckoned to her and swung open the gate.

Dalla followed him through it into a vast, oblong

courtyard. It was paved with wooden planks and brightly lit by more torches, burning in iron stands. Neat rows of thatched, wooden huts stood along three sides of it. In the middle was the King's Hall.

This Hall was as high as an oak tree. Its wooden walls were darkly oiled. Its tiled roof was deeply sloping and edged with two huge, curving white whalebones.

Brown Beard led Dalla under an open porch and through a heavy, richly carved oak door. Behind it was an entrance area full of hooks hung with expensive cloaks and fur hats. They went through a second door and emerged into a magnificent room.

Down each side of it there was a broad wall-bench, lavishly furnished with soft fur rugs and brightly coloured, tasselled cushions. Sumptuous tapestries and rows of highly polished weapons adorned the walls above them. Hundreds of oil lamps flickered in iron holders hanging by long chains from the ceiling. The fire-pit in the centre of the room had beautifully ornamented iron sides. Blazing flames leaped up from it.

The hall was crowded with men and women, all splendidly dressed, groomed and bejewelled. Some were standing around, talking and laughing. Some were lounging on the cushions and furs, nibbling snacks or swigging from elaborately decorated drinking-horns.

There wasn't another child in sight

Brown Beard pushed his way through the crush. Dalla followed him in a daze, dazzled by the brightness and warmth. Before she knew it, she was standing in front of the royal high-seats.

And what magnificent seats they were! They were fashioned from three different coloured woods: one pale, one middling brown and the third dark. The woods were all inlaid together and carved into twirling designs of Yggdrasill, the magic tree said to link the worlds of the gods, the people and the dead.

One of the high-seats was empty. On the other sat the beautiful woman Dalla had seen in the market place: Queen Gunnhild!

24

The Queen looked at Dalla through hawk-sharp, grey eyes. 'What do you want, you scruffy little urchin?' she said coldly.

Dalla stared nervously at the Queen's flowing, blue silken dress with its rows of rich embroidery and sparkling amber beads.

I must be careful! she thought. *Just in case she really is a witch.* She shuddered. *I mustn't say the wrong thing like I usually do. I mustn't annoy her. I've got to make her believe me. Aki and Frodi's lives depend on it!*

Brown Beard said, 'Excuse me bringing you such a revolting child, Your Majesty...'

'She stinks like a sewer mouse,' said the Queen.

'But she claims to know where that berserk has his hideout,' said Brown Beard.

'Do you now?' said the Queen. She leaned forward

thoughtfully, pressing together her fingers. They were clad in heavy gold and silver rings, with long nails like a wildcat's claws. 'Just a moment: haven't I seen you before somewhere? I recognise that scraggly mop of hair.'

'Please, Your Majesty, it was in the street near the marketplace,' said Dalla very politely.

'Ahah! The rascally girl with the impertinent brothers. What's your name?'

'Dalla Snorrisdaughter, Your Majesty.'

'Go on then, Dalla Snorrisdaughter, tell me what you know. And don't mumble.'

'Please, Your Majesty,' said Dalla, 'I know where the berserk is. I've seen him there. And he's captured both my brothers!'

'Pah!' cried the Queen. 'I put out a warning! I issued specific instructions not to trust the rogue. But did anyone listen? Did they pay regard to my years of learning and experience? No! Those ignorant townspeople thought they knew better than their wise and noble Queen. Well, don't expect any sympathy from me, girl. Your brothers have only themselves to blame.'

'But he's doing terrible things to them!' Dalla said.

'I'm not surprised.'

Make her understand! thought Dalla. *Surely I can do it!*

'He isn't a proper berserk,' she blurted out. 'That's a disguise. He's really Grim Gruesome!'

The Queen let out a furious splutter. 'Grim Gruesome? Troll bones! I shall strangle someone if I have to hear that country bumpkins' guff again! I've explained this a thousand times – is everyone deaf?'

She flicked her fingers at Dalla contemptuously, making her rings flash. Then she spoke very crisply and clearly as if Dalla were a simpleton:

'Grim … Gruesome … is … not … a … real … man... He's … made … up … A … fantasy! Odin's eye socket! I can't believe that people in a sophisticated town like Jorvik can fall for such ridiculous claptrap. The berserk is nothing more than a common liar, trickster and thief. Do you hear me girl? The only reason I care about him is that he has grievously insulted King Eirik Blood-Axe, my husband. And for that, I SHALL HAVE REVENGE!'

Several people turned round to see why the Queen was shouting. But when they realised she was only talking to an urchin child, they lost interest.

'Then can you…' said Dalla.

'Silence, girl! I am in the middle of planning important deeds. How dare you come and disturb me with your filthy rags and twaddle? Get out of my sight, Dalla Snorrisdaughter – before I really lose my temper!'

Dalla flinched. *Thunderbolts!* she thought. *She's going to put a spell on me!* But then she remembered that all this talk of the Queen being a witch was just lies invented by the berserk. *I can't let this chance go!* she thought.

'In the name of mighty Thor!' she cried. 'In the name of Odin All-Father! Your Majesty, I beg you to listen! I can tell you exactly where the berserk is hiding. You could send your soldiers there to destroy him tonight.' In her desperation, the words came spilling out. 'Along the road from the South-West Gate – down the fork into a forest to an old yew tree – follow the track behind it to the...'

'Enough!' Queen Gunnhild snarled.

Dalla bit her lip and stopped.

The Queen sat staring at her for a long moment through narrowed eyes. Then her lips twisted into a dangerous smile and she stood up.

'I think it is time to change my plans,' she said

softly. 'Ya, if you can find your way back to where the berserk is hiding, you will be useful. *Very* useful. Come!'

She waved Brown Beard out of the way. Then she took a small lamp from a stand, beckoned to Dalla and led her out through a side door.

25

Dalla followed Queen Gunnhild down a short, dark passage. At the end was another door. The Queen opened it and they stepped outside into the night. The Queen paused and blew out the lamp.

Silhouetted buildings and fences loomed darkly in the frosty moonlight: a silvery world without colour. The palace guards were all way off under the burning torches at the far end of the great courtyard. There was no one else around.

Dalla shivered.

The Queen walked briskly towards a wooden storage hut and opened its door with a small key.

'Wait here.'

She disappeared inside, then came out carrying a small soapstone dish and grinding stick, a silver spoon with an ornate walrus-ivory handle and a small bottle.

'Hold this.'

She thrust the bottle into Dalla's hand. It was made of clear glass, tapered at the bottom, curving out voluptuously, then narrowing to a slim neck. It was encircled in a coiled stand of delicate, black wrought iron, shaped to resemble a snake.

'Follow me.'

Behind the hut, in a shaft of moonlight, Dalla saw a small patch of earth. A low bush grew on it, beside the brittle, autumnal remains of many dead flowers. It smelled pungently of damp earth and mouldy leaves.

The Queen put the things she was carrying on top of a water barrel. She fetched a digging-stick that was propped against the wall. Her silk dress rustled in the stillness.

She pushed the stick into the ground and jiggled it about.

Soon she had dug out a small piece of root. She scooped it up with the silver spoon, dropped it into the soapstone dish and set to work on it with the grinding-stick. As Dalla watched, the root disintegrated into powder.

Now the Queen removed the lid from the barrel, scooped out some water with the spoon, poured it into the dish and stirred the mixture carefully.

'Give me the bottle.'

Heart thumping, Dalla handed it to her. She felt queasy and slightly dizzy.

The Queen poured the liquid from the dish into the bottle, taking great care not to spill it. The sound of it trickling seemed to fill the deserted courtyard. When it was done, she sealed the bottle with a wooden stopper. She held it out tantalisingly to Dalla, as if it contained something delicious.

The moon shone through the glass. The strange liquid seethed and frothed.

'What is it?' whispered Dalla.

'Oh come now, Dalla, work it out yourself,' said the Queen.

She's not a witch, Dalla told herself firmly. *So it can't be a magic brew. But what else could it be? – Oh!*

'Is it…?' she said fearfully, 'Is it…*poison?*'

26

'Wolfsbane,' said Queen Gunnhild. '*Deadly* poison. You must give it to the berserk, Dalla. Find a way to mix it secretly into his food.'

'Me?' Dalla gasped. Her voice rose to a scream: she couldn't help herself. 'B...b...but... Oh, I can't!' Her head was still full of that horrible, heart-stopping moment when the berserk had revealed himself as Grim Gruesome. 'I daren't go near him again!'

'What? Not even to save your brothers?' cried the Queen.

'But please, Your Majesty – surely it would be better for your soldiers to go and kill him?'

The Queen shook her head. 'A berserk in a fighting frenzy, can kill dozens of men at once. I'm not wasting...'

'But he isn't a real berserk,' Dalla interrupted her.

'Be quiet! I'm not wasting good soldiers on him, when you and I can easily outwit him with a simple trick.'

'But I can't...'

'Of course you can! You've already proved that you're bold and sharp-witted.'

Dalla stared at Queen Gunnhild in astonishment.

'You found the brute's hideout, and came back safely to report it,' said the Queen. 'You persuaded my guards to break strict orders and let you in. You're just the sort of person I need.'

Ooh! thought Dalla. *If only Mam and Aki could hear that!*

The Queen seized Dalla's hand and forced her to close her fingers around the little bottle. It felt cold and fragile.

If I hold it too tightly, she thought, *it'll break.*

'Take it,' said the Queen. 'Do it.'

27

Dalla crept home in the moonlight, clutching the bottle of poison gingerly in front of her. She was terrified she would drop it. She was terrified it would leak and contaminate her fingers.

But somehow she carried it safely back to the bucket shop at the end of Cupmakers' Street. She fumbled at her belt for the key and unlocked the door of the little house. Inside it was icy cold and completely dark.

She put the bottle carefully down on the floor and locked the door tightly behind her.

'Mam,' she whispered miserably. 'Pa. I wish you were here to look after me.'

And she imagined her mother scolding her in answer: '*In Thor's name, Dalla, act like the big girl you are. You're quite capable of lighting the fire and the lamps yourself!*'

Dalla sighed and felt her way through the gloom to the log basket. She carried a clutch of kindling twigs, dried grass and wood to the fire-pit. Then she felt along the shelves for the fire-making kit.

She'd never been trusted with it before. But tonight she had no choice. She opened the wooden box and pulled out the metal strike-a-light, the flint and a piece of touchwood. She scooped the grass and kindling twigs into a pile in the fire-pit. Then she moved the strike-a-light against the flint, until sparks flew up and the touchwood glowed. She blew it into a flame and lit the grass, which lit the kindling. Soon she'd got a fine log fire going, with yellow flames leaping up cheerfully.

By the firelight she found the jar of seal-oil, ladled some into the pottery lamps and lit them with a stick from the fire. The shadows retreated and it began to feel like home.

Dalla glanced across to the poison bottle. It gleamed in the firelight, filled with deadly power.

I can't do it, she thought. *Oh mighty Thor! Freyja, Lofn and Hlin and all you other goddesses who are supposed to answer prayers – help me! I can't go back to him. I can't murder him! I'm too young! That's a job for men, not girls!*

But the memory of what she had seen and heard in the forest came creeping back into her head:

'...you'll get the squirts and faint with horror...tear you apart, limb by limb...crave a taste of your pretty little sister...'

'Oh, but I've got to,' she cried aloud. 'Or he'll eat me! I can't bear it! And I'm so tired and hungry!'

Luckily she still had some honeycomb left and the mice hadn't come out to nibble it. She curled up on the wall-bench and started gulping it down.

She'd barely swallowed two mouthfuls before there came a raucous knocking on the door:

BAM! BAM! BAM!

Dalla froze. This is it! It's Grim Gruesome come for me! she thought. Her heart almost stopped with terror.

'Open up!' yelled a man's voice. 'King's soldiers!'

Soldiers? She relaxed a tiny bit. Why on earth are they knocking on our door? Are they after Aki and Frodi? Or...supposing it's HIM after all, just pretending...?

'We know you're in there!' came the voice. 'We can see the light shining. Open up by order!'

No, I'm sure that doesn't sound like him. I know, it must be those ruffians Mam once warned me about – the ones that go round playing tricks so they can break in and steal *things. Well, I'll never let them in. Thunderbolts! Why does this have to happen on top of everything else?*

Dalla kept her lips tightly shut. She hardly even breathed.

And at last the banging and yelling stopped.

She didn't fancy any more honeycomb. Its intense sweetness tangled with the knot in her stomach and made her feel sick. So she put the rest back on the shelf. Then she lay down on the bench, snuggled under some blankets and drifted into an exhausted sleep...

'Dalla!'

She sat bolt upright. *Who's calling my name?*

She listened. There it was again, a boyish voice outside:

'Dalla, it's me, Frodi. Open up!'

Her heart soared.

He's got free! she thought. *Oh, Thor be praised!*

She jumped up and ran to the door.

'Hurry up,' came the voice. 'I'm freezing out here!'

She began to turn the key...then stopped.

Something wasn't right.

It definitely sounded like Frodi. And yet... Frodi had a key with him. If he'd lost it, he would be worked up into a state and rattling the door. He'd be yelling, not calling out calmly.

If only she could peep outside and check if it was really him. But Viking houses didn't have windows.

Anyway, she thought, *Frodi's Grim Gruesome's prisoner. And once that villain catches you, it's impossible to escape!*

She yanked the key out of the lock and stepped back quickly.

I bet it's those those ruffians again. They know I'm on my own here. Supposing they break down the door? Oh, Thor help me!

She waited in a sweat of terror.

At last she heard footsteps walking away.

Wearily, she got back into bed. She was trembling all over.

But I've managed to get rid of them twice! she thought. *Queen Gunnhild would be proud of me!*

This comforted her a little and gave her courage. She tossed about restlessly for a short time, then managed to fall back to sleep.

She didn't wake until the cold hours just before dawn. Her stomach was rumbling.

I wish I had some proper food to eat, she thought.

And at that very moment, as if Thor himself had answered her prayers, she heard a woman in the street outside calling softly:

'Fresh-baked bread for sale! Still warm from the pan! Start the morning with my fine, fresh barley-bread. Wake up, slumber-heads! Three loaves for a quarter of a penny! Fresh-baked bread for sale!'

Dalla pushed off the covers and sat up. In the lamplight, the first thing she saw was the glass poison bottle, glinting on the floor by the door. Quickly, she looked away. She slid sleepily to her feet and went to look in the money-pot.

Ya! There were still six silver pennies left in it, plus several half-coins and quarter-coins. She grabbed one of the quarter-pennies, then hesitated.

Supposing it's the ruffians again? she thought. *But hold on, surely they wouldn't have a woman with them...*

The idea of fresh bread made her mouth water and her stomach rumble. She unlocked the door and ran outside.

Dalla's house was the very last one at the end of Cupmakers' Street. The bread-seller was standing in a shaft of moonlight, just a short way past it. She had her back to Dalla: a big woman, fat as a mother hen, wrapped against the night cold in a thick, hooded cloak. She was carrying a wooden pole, balanced across her shoulders. Several flat, brown loaves with holes in the middle were threaded onto either end.

'Please ma'am, I'll buy some bread!' called Dalla.

The seller didn't seem to hear her. *Perhaps she's a bit deaf,* thought Dalla. So she went up and touched the big woman's arm.

At once the woman turned round – and Dalla screamed.

For the loaf-pole was a sham. She could see now that the loaves were just bundles of dirty straw. It wasn't even a woman.

It was a huge, powerful man with a dark beard poking out from the deep shadows of his hood. His eyes were hidden. His whole face was hidden. But there was no doubting who he was.

'Dalla,' Grim Gruesome said softly, 'I saw you in the forest.'

Dalla's legs turned to water.

'You pathetic worm,' said Grim Gruesome. 'Surely you didn't believe you could escape me?'

28

Dalla turned and ran back to her house. Grim
Gruesome strode after her. She could run fast; but each
one of Grim Gruesome's steps was worth two or three
of hers. She reached home moments before him and
scuttled inside.

But before she could slam the door shut, he wedged
his great boot over the threshold and kept it there.
Dalla struggled with the door, using all her might to
try and push him back. But she was as weak against
him as a mouse against a giant.

'It would all be over much more quickly if you let
me in,' he hissed. 'Why prolong the agony, Dalla? Why
spin out the fear?'

He gave the door a ferocious kick. It crashed
painfully against her. She stumbled back – and Grim
Gruesome stormed in.

Dalla's blood ran cold. She backed away from him, clattering against the storage jars that stood along the wall by the door.

Grim Gruesome pushed the door shut. He was so enormous, he had to stoop under the low ceiling. He sat himself down on the end of a wall-bench, guarding the door. His foul stench filled the room. The heavy silence was broken only by the rasping of his breath. What horrors might be scored across his face, hidden as it always was, in the shadows of his hood?

The poison! thought Dalla.

The little bottle was still standing on the floor just inside the door. Heart in mouth, she snatched it up and clutched it behind her back. Then she sidled away to the opposite wall. She squeezed into the gap next to the big, upright weaving loom, trying to keep as far away from him as possible.

Grim Gruesome's hidden gaze bored through her.

'I am your guest, Dalla,' he said. 'Remember what Odin All-Father said: *"Do not chase your guest away."'* He gave a bellow of laughter. 'You must make me welcome and look after me. I am hungry, Dalla: I am ravenous! Get me something to eat.'

'I...I...I'm afraid all I've got is a bit of honeycomb,'

whispered Dalla.

'Then give me that.'

Grim pulled off his great, furry gloves and held out his left hand. The lamp-light flickered and danced on his finger-stump. It was black and swollen, crusted with a thick scum of dried yellow pus.

Dalla retched.

She shifted the poison bottle into the folds of her apron and went to the low shelf where she'd left the wooden platter of half-eaten honeycomb. She kept her back to Grim Gruesome and slipped the bottle onto the shelf.

Maybe I could pour the poison onto the honey without him noticing, she thought.

Her hand went back to the bottle.

Freyja's tears! But I can't kill anyone – not even him!

'Hurry up!' Grim Gruesome growled at her. 'What are you doing?'

'I...um nothing,' she whispered.

'You're hiding something, aren't you Dalla?'

'N...n...no sir!'

'Bring it to me!' Grim Gruesome roared.

His rasping voice filled the room like smoke. It was impossible to refuse him. Trembling from head to toe,

Dalla crept across to him and held out the plate of honeycomb and the bottle.

Grim Gruesome snatched them both from her. Her hand smarted and tingled from the touch of his coarse fingertips. He put the plate down. He held the bottle up under his hood, pulled out the stopper and sniffed it.

'Hmmm,' he said. 'So your father has a taste for foreign boozy drinks, does he? Fancy a mere bucket-maker being able to afford a fine, spiced mead like this. Haven't you got any manners, girl? You should give your guest the best of everything.' He laughed again. 'Why didn't you offer this to me?'

'I...I...I...' stuttered Dalla. She felt sick with terror.

Grim Gruesome made a loud, lip-smacking noise. He crammed the whole hunk of honeycomb into the shadows under his hood. In the stillness of the room, Dalla heard him chewing noisily and swallowing. A sticky stream of honey and saliva dribbled down the bristly fronds of his beard.

Then he threw back his head so that Dalla could just make out the angular shape of his face. The darkness of his open mouth was like a bottomless hole. He put the bottle to it and poured the poison straight down his throat.

29

Dalla waited for him to gag and screech with pain.

But instead Grim Gruesome wiped his mouth with his deformed left hand and patted his belly.

'By Odin!' he rasped. 'That's a fine, blood-warming brew!'

He stood up, went to the door and beckoned to her.

Dalla didn't move. She held her breath and waited for the poison to work.

But Grim Gruesome just seemed brawnier and more savage than ever. He heaved the door wide open, letting in a shaft of grey dawn light. He strode back into the room – and made a grab for Dalla.

She ducked, dodged him and ran out into the street. Grim Gruesome came after her.

There was a clear sky and a full moon. Dalla raced through the cold dawn.

Get to the palace square! she thought. *The King's soldiers will save me!*

But Grim Gruesome strode straight past her. Halfway along Cupmakers' Street, he stopped and held his monstrous arms wide open, blocking her way.

Dalla had never thought or acted so quickly before. She skidded to a halt, turned back on herself, squeezed between the fences of two house-yards and came out onto Ouse Street. You could reach the palace that way too. But Grim Gruesome was already there to stop her.

Dalla turned on her heels again and ran frantically, hopelessly, down the slope towards the river.

As she ran, she screamed. But there were no houses along the riverbank, only warehouses, deserted at this time. Besides, people were always screaming in the night in Jorvik and nobody ever took any notice. Her side was knotted up with a painful stitch, but she didn't dare stop.

Not onto the bridge! she thought. *Not to the gate that leads to his hideout!*

She swerved onto King Street. *Round the block... Get to the palace that secret way...*

In the dark, her eyes were skinned for an alley she knew. But Grim Gruesome was just a breath behind her, huge in his billowing cloak.

'I see you, Dalla!' he roared. His voice was deep as a grave, melting into a wolf-howl.

Dalla's blood turned to ice. She hesitated, teetering in the middle of the road. Cold grey light was seeping into the sky. With it came the eerie neighing of a horse.

She held her breath and listened. Hooves came pounding along the beaten-mud street.

And suddenly the horse appeared.

It came cantering down King Street, straight towards her. It was an enormous creature, black as midnight. Its mane and tail streamed as it moved, like flowing strands of fine-spun silver. It was surely the same horse she had seen the day before, the one that led her into the forest.

For a brief moment she felt a pang of hope. *If I could somehow climb on its back, it might carry me away to safety*, she thought. *Or maybe it'll get in the way of Grim Gruesome so I can escape...*

But Grim Gruesome gave a shout: 'Here, Haski! Come here my beauty!'

And Haski neighed again, tossed his head and cantered straight past Dalla. He stopped in front of Grim Gruesome, his master. He waited.

Grim flung back his cloak and leaped onto Haski's bare back. He leaned forward and whispered strange words – gibberish – into the horse's ear. He jabbed his boots into the creature's flank. The horse turned and came, at a gallop now, back towards Dalla.

Everything's over, thought Dalla. *I'm finished.*

Her legs were weak and shaking. All the fight had drained out of her. She couldn't run any more. She didn't try to dodge away. She just stood there, swaying, half-swooning, staring in horror. Haski bore down on her, carrying Grim Gruesome on his back.

As they came level, Grim bent down, grasped Dalla under the armpits and swept her up in front of him. His iron grip seemed to squeeze her through to her bones. His breath burned into the back of her neck. She felt the smoothness and warmth of the horse's back beneath her. The world spun. The dawn light hazed and shimmered. Dalla screwed up her eyes and grabbed fearfully at the horse's silvery mane.

The last thing she saw was the town gate. She heard a blood-curdling shriek as Grim Gruesome disposed of its watchman. The gate stood wide open. They passed through it like a hurricane. And then she fainted.

30

Later that same morning, at Grim Gruesome's lair in the forest, Aki slowly surfaced from a long, suffocating sleep. He opened his eyes. All he could see was impenetrable darkness.

He lay very still. A nauseating smell of animal droppings and damp wool filled his nostrils. He felt stiff all over. He seemed to be lying in an awkward, unnatural position.

Mighty Thor! he thought. His heart began to pound violently. *Farting giantesses! It can't be true...* He dozed and jerked suddenly awake again. *But I think it must be. Ya, Grim Gruesome's really done what he threatened. He's... he's turned me into a* sheep!

He retched violently and began to tremble. His whole being sagged with the horror of it.

Thor help me! I feel so stupid! The other lads would

laugh me into the ground if they knew. Thunderbolts! But how would *they even know? All they'd see is a pathetic, bleating animal – they'd never even guess it was me. What in Thor's name am I going to do?*

His head ached and stung as if his scalp and brains had been gouged out with a knife. *Aw no! That must be where my...* He swallowed a mouthful of vomit. *Where my sheep's horns have grown,* he thought bleakly.

In the dark, all alone with no one to see his cowardice, he wanted to cry.

Farting giantesses! I don't suppose I can even make tears, with sheep's eyes.

He became aware of tight lumps at the ends of his legs.

Hooves!

Tentatively, he tried knocking one of the front ones against the floor. The movement seemed to make the lump dissolve. To his surprise, it loosened and uncurled.

But my fingers – they're still there!

They felt twisted and strange. Heart in mouth, Aki tried moving them over himself, expecting to find sheep's wool beneath them. Instead he touched coarse cloth...and smooth human skin.

My clothes. My own skin!

Under his touch, his head felt like his own too. There were gashes and clots of dried blood in his hair, but no sign of horns.

Then he realised the foul smell wasn't actually him. It came from a filthy sheepskin flung across his body. He tossed it off. Slowly, he managed to sit up.

He felt confused and disorientated. He was desperately thirsty. His head was throbbing badly.

He blinked in the darkness.

Just now, he thought dazedly. *While I slept...Was I really a sheep...? Or did I just imagine it? But no. Those weird words he chanted... That horrible finger-stump...!*

A vivid memory of Grim Gruesome's threats and spells came rushing back at Aki. With it came a fresh wave of shivers and nausea. In his mind's eye he saw again how Grim had waved his finger-stump before him like an oversized, pus-filled maggot. It had sent him into a trance, filled with Grim's putrid body-stink, smothering Aki in a furnace of evil, shape-shifting magic.

Was it just a nightmare? he wondered. *No, no it was too real. But then the magic...must have worn off?*

Relief overwhelmed him. He stood up shakily,

stretched and flexed his arms. He squatted down then straightened up again. Strength and feeling rushed back into his limbs.

But where am I?

'Hello?' he called into the blackness. 'Is anybody there?'

Only silence answered him. He held his hand in front of his eyes, but it was so dark he couldn't see it at all.

Get away from here before he comes back! he thought. *No time to lose!*

He held his hands out before him and moved unsteadily forward. One step. Two. Three... Suddenly his fingers grazed against a rough stone wall. Keeping close, he shuffled carefully along it.

After a while, one hand bumped against something metal. *Something must be hanging up here,* he thought.

He stopped. Blindly, tentatively, he explored each item. A huge sword in a scabbard. A very large fur cloak. A farmer's scythe for cutting corn. A leather bag. An axe with a wooden handle.

Carefully he unhooked the axe. Then he unhooked the sword and pulled it from its scabbard. They were much heavier than any weapons he'd held before. He propped them on the ground by his feet while his hands examined the fur.

This could be useful too. If I ever manage to get out of here, I might have to sleep rough. It would keep me warm...

But when he pulled at it, the fur gave off that horrible stink of rotting meat that Grim Gruesome had about him.

Pshaw! It must be his bearskin!

Aki left it where it was.

He grasped the sword in one hand and the axe in the other, panting a little at their weight. Then he shouldered his way on along the wall.

Abruptly the stone gave way to wood. He saw a crack of light, fine as a spider's thread. The door!

He put the weapons down and felt the door carefully all over. He found a keyhole – but no key. He found two large iron hinges. There was no handle, no latch.

He's locked me in here, the brute! Anger surged through him, giving him strength.

Well: I'll break my way out!

He picked up the axe with both hands, stepped back and practiced swatting it through the murky air. Once he'd got the knack, he felt his way back to the door and swung the axe against it.

THWACK! The wood was very old and half rotten. It started to give way at once. Encouraged, he smashed the axe at it over and over again. Eventually a hole appeared. Daylight!

Aki was weak with relief. He pushed his head through the splinters, blinking and breathing in great gasps of fresh air. His head cleared. The forest stood before him. The day was bright.

I'm still alive, he thought, *I'm still me!*

He hacked at the door some more until the hole was large enough to clamber through. He dropped to the ground. And at once he heard someone whimper.

31

'Help, help!' came the voice. It sounded weak and feeble, but Aki recognised it instantly.

'Frodi!' he cried in astonishment. 'Farting giantesses! How did *you* get here?'

There was a long silence. Then Frodi called fearfully,

'Aki? Is that...*you*?'

'Ya, it's me. Where are you, Frodi?'

'But he said... Grim Gruesome... He said he'd transformed you into a sheep!'

Aki shuddered and tried to swallow the unbearable memory of it. 'He did,' he called back. 'But it seems to have worn off. I...I think I'm normal now. Where are you?'

'In the ruined bit. Grim Gruesome chucked me in here and and tied me up.'

'Hold on there, Frodi, I'm coming.'

Aki ran shakily towards the sound of his brother's voice. In the tumbledown half of the building he saw the remains of a door hanging loose in its frame. He pushed his way through and found himself staring into an old cattle byre.

The floor was littered with dirty straw and fallen stones. Frodi had been chucked into the remains of a feeding trough. He was trussed up in coarse ropes, like a pig ready to be roasted on the spit. Aki picked his way across to him.

'I'm frozen,' Frodi groaned. 'He left me out here in the cold all night. He said it would soften me up for his spells.'

'Well, he's farting well not putting any more spells on us now,' said Aki stoutly.

He pulled the knife from his belt and cut carefully through the ropes.

Frodi wriggled his arms and legs. He was almost as stiff as a dead body. Aki helped him to his feet.

'I can hardly move,' said Frodi.

'You've got to!' Aki retorted. 'I felt just as bad as you – no, worse! – a short time ago. We can't hang around. Tell me quickly: do you know where Grim Gruesome is?'

'He went off on his horse to...'

'Come on then!' urged Aki. 'Let's get out before he comes back!'

He took Frodi's arm and began to lead him across the rubble.

'No, no, listen!' cried Frodi. He could only walk very awkwardly and he was shivering violently. 'Grim Gruesome's gone off on his horse to snatch Dalla! He's going to bring her *here*! That's what he said.'

'Aw, pig turds and dwarf spit!' swore Aki.

'We're trapped, Aki,' said Frodi wretchedly. 'We'll have to wait here until he comes back with her. We've got to try and save her!'

The two boys stood there uncertainly, white faced, wobbling on numb legs, clutching each other. They gazed down the narrow track that led away into the forest.

'Perhaps we'd best go back to town and get help,' said Aki. 'Go to the palace and tell them we've found Grim Gruesome. Then they'll send soldiers.'

'But they won't,' said Frodi. 'Queen Gunnhild will never let them. She's put out a proclamation saying that Grim Gruesome is just made-up stories, that he doesn't even exist.'

'But that's ridiculous! We've seen him! He caught us!'

'Ya, ya I know… But that's what *she* believes. Anyway, even if we could get back to town quickly and some soldiers came straight out here – it would probably still be too late to save Dalla.'

Aki sighed and leaned wearily against the wall.

'All right, Frodi,' he said. 'You suggest something.'

'Me?' said Frodi stupidly. 'But you're the oldest. You're always in charge.'

'Ya,' Aki muttered gloomily. 'And I got us all into this stupid mess. Help me think how to get out of it. Come on, how can we rescue Dalla from the brute?'

Frodi swallowed. 'Well. Um…we could hide in the trees?' he said. 'When Grim Gruesome comes back along the track with Dalla, we could jump out at him…'

'Don't be stupid,' said Aki. 'You've seen Grim Gruesome yourself, Frodi, you've had a taste of his evil, you know how strong he is. We wouldn't stand a chance against him.'

Frodi flushed. 'Well, I don't know what else to suggest. If you really want my opinion, Aki, I...I'd give that a try...If we could only find something to use as weapons.'

'Weapons!' cried Aki. 'I almost forgot. Come and see!'

He took Frodi round to the broken-down door and showed him the axe and the sword. Frodi's eyes almost popped out of his head.

'Oh wow. *Wow,* Aki, just look at them! That's a really, really fine sword.'

Aki hesitated. He swallowed. 'Go on then, Frodi,' he said. 'You take that.'

'Me?' said Frodi. 'Are you sure?'

'I can do just as much damage with the axe,' said Aki. 'Look how sharp it is. Come on, we ought to set up our ambush as fast as we can, in case he suddenly appears.'

Frodi gripped the sword fiercely, relishing its weight. He kept glancing down at it, scarcely able to believe that he was actually holding it in his own hand.

They carried the weapons into the forest, stopping at a stream to gulp down refreshing mouthfuls of water. Further along, they found a small clearing screened by large trees and brambles, with a good view of the track.

'Shh!' hissed Frodi suddenly. 'Someone's coming!'

They stood side by side, listening.

A horse was clip-clopping steadily along the track, getting closer.

Aki put a finger to his lips.

The horse's hooves were nearly upon them. The brothers peered out from the shelter of a holly bush, clasping their weapons. They saw Haski cantering towards them along the narrow path. They could just make out a huge, dark shape on his back.

'Ready?' Aki whispered.

Fearfully, Frodi nodded.

Haski was almost level with them. They could clearly see now that Grim Gruesome was riding him, towering above them in his billowing, deep-hooded cloak. In front of him slumped a small human body.

'Now!' cried Aki.

Brandishing their weapons, the two boys leaped out into the open.

32

Haski reared up. His mane flared out, shimmering like threads of silver in the dull autumn light. Grim Gruesome leaped from the saddle and flung back his cloak. The boys saw his two swords hanging in heavily ornamented scabbards at his sides.

Grim rolled up his sleeves. His burn-blistered arm was almost the colour of blood. His scabby finger-stump twitched. He drew both swords, one in each hand. Then he strode towards them, shoulders hunched, head thrust forward like a wild beast about to pounce.

Aki and Frodi glanced at each other. They'd both done plenty of mock fighting, but neither had ever fought a real battle. And the weapons they held were huge and cumbersome, meant for full-grown men, not boys. They peered hopelessly into the impenetrable shadows of Grim's hood, but as always, it was impossible to see the villain's face or where his eyes were looking.

Suddenly Grim Gruesome came rushing at them. One sword waved wildly around at Aki. The other pointed straight at Frodi's heart!

Frodi raised his own sword and struck back with it, falteringly but bravely. Then he darted out of the way. Grim Gruesome swung round and lunged at him again...

Aki ducked under Grim's other sword, came up behind Grim and smashed the axe hard against the villain's right boot.

For a brief moment Grim lost his footing. But his boots were tough as whale skin, and the blow scarcely hurt him at all. He twisted back and thwacked a sword-blade into Aki's forearm.

Aki gave a yelp of pain. Blood spurted from the wound and he dropped the axe. Grim Gruesome kicked it away with a pitiless bellow of laughter and tensed to strike Aki again.

But now Frodi had run behind him. He struck his sword at Grim's back with all his might. Grim jolted awkwardly – then at once swung round and hit back at him with his own double-handed sword blows. Frodi fought with incredible strength for such a young boy, but Grim was tall and strong as a frost-giant. And one sword against two was impossible.

Aki sucked at his wound, watching them through a mist of excruciating pain and despair. *He's going to kill Frodi any minute now!* he thought. *Farting giantesses, I can't let my own brother die!*

He gritted his teeth, took a deep breath and dived to the ground. Somehow he retrieved the axe in his good hand – came up beside Aki – and lurched at Grim under the billowing cloak.

He caught the brute's thigh. Grim reeled back with a roar. But almost at once he recovered. Now the brothers faced him together, side by side, as he lashed out at them again.

'You little teasers!' Grim Gruesome jeered.

His two swords flashed through the air like snakes of lightning. But his breath had turned into ugly, rattling gasps and his voice was slurred with the effort: it was hard to make out what he said.

'You're working me up an appetite before I devour you, eh? Mmm, delicious! Ha! You will taste all the better in a sauce of your own spilled blood. And see my friends, I have another little trick for you.'

In two strides, he was back at his horse. Now they saw that it was Dalla lashed onto the front of the saddle. She was panting furiously and wriggling, trying to loosen the hairy ropes that held her there.

Grim Gruesome thrust one of the swords away into its scabbard. He fondled Haski's muzzle with his hideous, four-fingered hand. Then with the other sword, he sliced through the ropes and pulled Dalla off like a sack of flour.

'You forgot about your little sister,' he rasped. 'But I didn't. You thought she was nice and safe in that cosy little house of yours with the door locked – but I easily plucked her out of it!'

He belched loudly and fell into a fit of coughing and retching. '*Blaagh*! *Yerch*!' He staggered around as if he were drunk. Then suddenly he dragged Dalla away from the horse and held her straight in front of him.

'How do you like my new shield, eh?'

He shook her hard. Dalla squealed.

'Your little sister is my protection,' he slurred. His voice had sunk to a low, gravelly hiss. 'Look at her: she's better than wood, better even than iron! So you think you can kill me, do you? You fools, don't you realise that I am invincible! Go on, Frodi, have another try at attacking me. But you'll have to drive your sword through *her* first.'

He began to twitch and belch again, his spittle dribbling onto Dalla's hair.

'Ya, Aki, you too, you cocky, self-important fool! The only way to kill me is by striking your axe through your own sister's heart!'

33

The moment stretched out.

Grim Gruesome loomed before the dark, dead-leafed forest, clasping Dalla with his hideous finger-stump clamped against her waist. In his other hand he brandished a sword. His breath came in loud, unearthly rasps.

'Bull turds and thunderbolts!' groaned Aki.

'Shall we try and wrestle him?' whispered Frodi. His lips scarcely moved.

'Good thinking!' Aki hissed back at him. 'One on each side. I'll count to three. Then grab his elbows...'

Frodi nodded. They were both on fire with tension: every muscle taut, minds as sharp as knives. They let their weapons drop. Aki began to count under his breath:

'One. Two. Three – CHARGE!'

They rushed at Grim Gruesome, shadows spinning before their eyes. Grim's sword swung round at them. His huge boot lashed out. But both boys ducked and dodged him, darting behind his back. Grim twisted round, loosening his grip on Dalla.

Aki saw his chance. He grabbed the huge arm that held his sister and tried to pull it away with all his might. It was like a slab of rock; but slowly, slowly it seemed to shift down under Aki's grip... Just as, from the other side, Grim's sword came slicing down through the air towards him!

In the instant before the sword could reach Aki, Frodi leaped up and smashed his clenched fist into Grim's exposed armpit. It was enough to make the brute lose momentum. Aki hurled himself out of the way. Dalla slid from Grim Gruesome's grip and tumbled to the ground with a startled shriek.

'Get up, Dalla!' yelled Frodi. 'In Thor's name – run!'

She stumbled up, dazed and trembling – collapsed onto her knees, shook back her tangle of hair – and began to crawl away towards the trees.

Grim Gruesome was roaring and howling as if he had really shape-shifted into a wild beast. He fumbled at his belt for the second sword, but he didn't seem able to draw it. Instead he staggered and turned about, this way, that way...

The boys had both sneaked behind him now. They counted down again – then rushed at him, heads down like charging bulls. As one, they smashed into his backside.

Grim's massive, iron-hard body jolted forward. He let out a gut-chilling shriek. Haski reared up with a whinny; then bolted away towards the ruin and the thicket of trees behind it.

'Aw, farting giantesses, look out!' yelled Frodi. 'He's spewing up!'

They scurried out of the way.

Grim Gruesome was standing in the path, heaving and spluttering. From under his hood, out shot a jet of dark, blood-stained vomit.

Then he started stampeding madly about the clearing – stumbling into the undergrowth, kicking up great splatters of mud, lashing out blindly with his two swords.

'Hateful children!' he rasped. 'Scum! Maggots! I shall tear you apart and gob...gob...gobble you up!' The words were slurred and misshapen, like a drunkard's. 'I shall shift your shapes into ssslug-wormzzz...'

He lurched violently forward and gagged out another stream of vomit. Then his legs buckled. His two swords clattered to the ground and he collapsed slowly on top of them.

'Smash into him while he's down!' yelled Aki.

Grim's hood enveloped his head like a shroud. His enormous body was jerking and twitching like a weird thing. The two boys snatched up their weapons...

'Aki!' shrieked Dalla, 'Frodi! Look – we've got help!'

They glanced round. Dalla was leaning weakly against the pale trunk of a birch tree, staring down the deer track. A band of soldiers was coming along it.

There were dozens of them, all on horseback. They wore the black-trimmed, scarlet tunics of the King's army and were heavily armed. Their swords flashed as they hacked their way through the undergrowth.

At their head rode a broad-shouldered man with a grey beard. He wore a gleaming chain-mail tunic and a shiny metal helmet decorated with a huge crest.

It was King Eirik Blood-Axe.

34

King Eirik sat majestically on his horse. He gazed round in silence at the three dishevelled, blood-stained children.

'You!' He snapped his fingers at Aki. 'Does this path lead to the hideout of the wretch who insulted me – the berserk?'

Aki drew himself up tall. 'Ya, Your Majesty,' he said breathlessly.

'Take me to him,' said the King. 'I've come here to kill him.'

'You're too late,' said Aki.

The King's face turned purple with fury. 'Who are you, impudent boy? One of the berserk's cronies, I suppose. And these other urchins...' He snapped his fingers at the soldiers. 'Seize all three of them!'

Several men jumped from their horses and rushed

to grab the children.

'Leave off!' cried Aki.

A soldier had him in an arm-lock. Aki twisted about in a fury to be free. 'I'm trying to tell you, we've killed Grim...him...the berserk...already! Look.'

He pointed behind him at the enormous body sprawled on the ground.

King Eirik grunted. He rode over to the body and stared down at it.

'This stinking corpse can't be the berserk,' he sputtered. 'I heard he always wore a bearskin cloak.'

'He did,' said Aki. 'I'll fetch it. I'll prove it's him!'

The King signalled to the soldier to free him. Aki skirted carefully round King Eirik's horse and Grim Gruesome's body. He ran back along the path. King Eirik followed.

At the ruined house, the King dismounted. Aki clambered in through the broken door. A broad shaft of light shone through it, clearly showing the cramped room where he'd been imprisoned. It was bare and derelict, almost completely empty. There were no wall-benches, no other pieces of furniture – just a crumbling stone fire-pit in the centre of the floor, heaped up with ancient charcoal and ashes.

There were the hooks he'd found before, with the scythe and the leather bag still hanging in place. Beside them was the monstrous bearskin cloak.

Its smell was overpowering. Aki gagged. Then he heaved it down, dragged it outside and laid it carefully at King Eirik's feet. Its eye sockets stared up eerily above the evil-looking fangs.

The King prodded it with the tip of his sword. Then he led the way back to the body.

'It seems this really is the treacherous brute,' he said. 'But berserks are said to have supernatural powers. By Odin, boy, how did you find the strength to kill him?'

'Oh please, Your Majesty, it was me!' cried Dalla. 'I gave him…'

Frodi trod hard on her foot. 'Shut up with your idiotic nonsense!' he hissed furiously. 'Don't you realise? This is the *King*!'

'It was me and my brother together, sir,' said Aki. 'And…ya, the berserk *did* have supernatural powers. But not in the way you mean.' He hesitated, trying to find words to convince the sceptical, world-weary King. 'The bearskin cloak was just a disguise. He was much more evil than you think. You see, he was really Grim…'

But the King wasn't listening. He was watching the dead body with grisly fascination. It was still twitching every so often, almost jumping into the air.

'Leave it until the death tremors have finished,' he said to his soldiers. 'No one will disturb it here. Come back tomorrow and bury it deep.

'So! Back to Jorvik, men! We'll take these children with us. Let's spread the news that my enemy is dead.'

35

Aki, Frodi and Dalla travelled back through the green farmlands of the Viking kingdom in high style. They rode in procession with the King's army, each one behind a soldier on horseback.

It was late afternoon by the time they reached Jorvik. The King led his soldiers ceremoniously through the gate, up Great Street and over the bridge. News of the berserk's killing ran ahead of them and spilled out through the narrow streets.

'Have you heard?' people cried. 'The berserk is dead!'

They came crowding noisily out of their houses and workshops to watch the King ride by.

'Dead?' others cried in dismay. 'But he was meant to save our children! What'll happen now if Grim Gruesome turns up?'

'Thor help us! It's no good looking to King Eirik Chicken-Heart to save us!'

'Exactly! But why are those two Snorrisson lads riding in the procession?'

'Look, their sister's there too – the little mischief maker!'

'They were conniving with the berserk, weren't they?'

'Ya, Eirik Blood-Axe must have caught the children with him and taken them prisoners...'

Prisoners? Huh! Those ignorant people should have seen what really happened when the King led Dalla, Frodi and Aki into the courtyard of the palace!

A swift-footed messenger had already carried the good news to Queen Gunnhild. She came hurrying out of the King's hall to meet them.

'Is it true that the berserk is dead?' she asked.

'Dead as a lump of stone,' King Eirik answered.

'Excellent!' cried the Queen. Her stern face softened into a look of triumph. 'A feast is already prepared to mark your return from pirating with three ships full of treasure, my lord. And now the berserk is destroyed, it'll be an even grander celebration.'

She clapped her hands. At once servants and slaves came running from all directions. The Queen shouted orders at them, naming long lists of foods. Then she turned her cold grey eyes to the horses and soldiers that had come up behind the King. She didn't seem at all surprised to see the three children amongst them.

'Dalla Snorrisdaughter,' she said. Her piercing gaze made Dalla blush. 'I was expecting you. Come here.'

The soldier mounted in front of Dalla helped her down from the horse. She stumbled wearily up to the Queen.

'Please, Your Majesty,' she said, 'I didn't actually give that…'

'Silence!' Queen Gunnhild interrupted her. 'You're filthy!'

'I don't know what this little urchin was up to when I found her in the forest,' said King Eirik. 'Tagging after these two lads, I suppose…' He gestured to Aki and Frodi. '…and getting in their way. But despite her, these lads… Hmm… they managed to play an important part in the berserk's death.'

Frodi raised his eyebrows at Aki. 'Isn't he going to say it was us who killed him?' he whispered.

'Shh,' Aki murmured. 'I suppose a king always has

to take the glory. Never mind. The main thing is, the deed is done.'

'They deserve to come to the feast,' the King said. 'Come forward, boys. Greet my Queen!'

Aki and Frodi both jumped down from their horses, walked up to Queen Gunnhild and bowed politely.

The Queen nodded and turned back to Dalla. 'Their sister must join us too,' she said. For a brief moment, her eyes crinkled and a knowing smile seemed to play about her lips.

Dalla flushed. She scratched herself. She pointed down at her torn, mud-stained dress.

'Please, Your Majesty,' she said, 'we haven't any better clothes.'

'Then we shall find you some,' the Queen said at once. 'But first you must be...' she shuddered, 'cleaned up.' She clapped her hands again. 'Where are those wretched house slaves?'

Two sharp faced slave-women with plain brown dresses and very short cropped hair came hurrying up.

'Take these youngsters into the bathhouse,' said Queen Gunnhild, 'and make sure they're all scrubbed thoroughly.'

The slaves led the three children outside into a

private corner of the courtyard. There they made all three of them undress – and then started whipping them hard with prickly bundles of twigs! Next they pushed the children into a dark hut filled with sizzling-hot steam, went out and locked the door.

In the sweltering darkness, Dalla whimpered.

'This is as bad as what Grim Gruesome did!' moaned Frodi.

'No it isn't,' said Aki. 'I've heard that noble folk do it every week.'

Just as they thought they would faint from the heat, the slaves opened the door, led them outside and drenched them in buckets of icy water!

Then they were taken into another hut, dried with soft linen cloths and each given a set of astonishingly fine clothes to put on. For the boys there were baggy trousers, braid-trimmed tunics, leather belts with ornamented bronze buckles, and boots of thick ox-hide. Dalla got a beautiful, pale-green dress woven from softest lambswool, a pink linen apron held up by real silver shoulder-brooches and a set of sparkly glass beads.

The slaves bowed and went out. Courtly servants came to fetch the three children and lead them into the

King's Hall.

Feasting tables had been set up along the cushioned wall-benches, laid with brimming dishes of meat and fruit. There was roasted duck, goose, pork, beef and venison, salted and pickled fish of every kind, oysters, stewed plums, richly coloured cold soups of elderberries, blackberries and rowan berries, and big pots of thick cream.

King Eirik and Queen Gunnhild were sitting majestically side by side on the high-seats, surrounded by elegantly dressed warriors and ladies. The Queen was wearing a deep crimson, pleated dress trimmed with gold and silver thread. The King wore a tunic of dark green velvet. He beckoned as the children came in.

He ignored Dalla, but led Aki and Frodi to a table surrounded by soldiers. Amongst them was Brown Beard from the marketplace. He seemed to know already that the boys had fought the berserk. He stood up, and offered them each a real drinking horn of beer.

'These two lads have the talent to become excellent warriors,' said King Eirik. 'Let them sit with you and listen to your talk.'

He turned to the two boys. 'At the end of the

evening, you can tell me if you want to train as soldiers and join my army.'

Frodi's mouth dropped open. 'Oh wow!' he cried. 'Both of us, Your Majesty? Not just Aki? Me as well?'

Aki grinned at him.

'Definitely!' they said together.

Brown Beard laughed. 'I'd think about it carefully, if I were you,' he said. 'Don't imagine a soldier's life is all excitement and glory. It's farting well dangerous most of the time. You'll most likely end up bleeding to death with a spear in your heart or your head sliced off with a sword.'

Aki nodded solemnly. The soldiers moved up to make room for the boys on the bench. King Eirik left them there and went off to mingle with his court.

Meanwhile, Dalla stood nervously by the high-seats, waiting for Queen Gunnhild to notice her.

36

'Sit there,' said the Queen at last. She pointed to the wall-bench next to her high-seat.

Dalla perched awkwardly on it. She wriggled around to get comfortable on a plump cushion of yellow silk. Even with the cushion, the bench was rather low and she was rather short: she could only just reach up to eat from the top table that stood in front of it. The Queen sat languorously beside her.

'Eat,' she said.

Dalla nodded. She helped herself to a golden-roasted duck leg dripping with fat, and started chewing at it greedily.

The Queen leaned across and murmured in a low voice: 'So: you gave him the poison?'

Dalla put the duck leg down quickly. A little puddle of fat dripped from it, seeping into her beautiful pink apron.

'Oh...ya, Your Majesty,' she said. 'Well, that is...I...I didn't actually *give* it to him... He came to our house, you see, and...I was going to try... But then he snatched it and swallowed it anyway.'

'Ah, so you hide your bravery behind a mask of modesty,' said the Queen approvingly. 'Very cunning. But you can be open with me, Dalla. We both know that the berserk is only dead because you and I dealt with him.' To Dalla's surprise, the Queen gave a little chuckle. 'But we will keep that as our secret, eh?'

'Ya, Your Majesty,' said Dalla. *Lucky I never got the chance to tell the King,* she thought.

'But it didn't work,' she said aloud. 'After he swallowed the poison, nothing happened. That's when he caught me! He tied me up and carried me away to the forest. He was still perfectly all right when Aki and Frodi started fighting him.'

'Indeed,' said the Queen.

Dalla shuddered. A bitter lump rose in her throat at the memory, but she swallowed it quickly and sneaked another bite of duck. 'He was so horrible. It's true what I told you, Your Majesty. He wasn't just a berserk – he was really Grim Gruesome!'

'The bigger the lie, the more people seem to believe it,' the Queen said drily. 'I assure you, Dalla, Grim Gruesome is not a real man. The berserk was the only villain – and now we all know for sure that he is dead. Here, taste this.'

She offered a dish of oysters, but Dalla wrinkled her nose with frustration and shook her head.

'Of course nothing happened at once when you gave the berserk the poison,' the Queen went on. 'You didn't expect it to be instant, did you? It needs time to seep through the body and destroy it. King Eirik tells me that the brute's corpse was lying in a mess of vomit. That's a sure sign that the poison had worked.'

Dalla was getting more and more confused. 'But he was perfectly all right until Aki and Frodi fought him,' she said.

The Queen laughed. 'Ya, your brothers are a couple of bold young stags, that's for sure. But they didn't realise our little secret, did they? They had no idea they were fighting a man who was already dying! And that was thanks to me and *you*, Dalla. Berserks are notoriously hard to kill: he'd have put up a much tougher battle and probably killed both your brothers before the King arrived, if you hadn't got the poison into him. Well done!'

Dalla blushed bright red. The Queen was the first person who had ever praised her in all her life.

'You know, I like you, Dalla Snorrisdaughter,' said Queen Gunnhild. 'I like your boldness. I can tell you think your own thoughts. So let me give you some good advice. Whenever you find yourself in a dangerous situation, remember this: Woman's cunning can always beat man's brute strength.'

Dalla was too overcome to speak. *The Queen likes me!* she thought.

Queen Gunnhild reached out to the table for a brimming bowl of berry soup. She ladled some cream into it and began spooning it into her mouth.

'When we have finished eating,' she said, 'I will give you your reward.'

37

By the time the King and Queen sent Aki, Frodi and Dalla home, it was well past midnight. They were all bone-weary, but bursting with good food and bubbling with excitement.

No torches were burning in the narrow streets of Jorvik. No stars or moon shone that night to light their way. Everyone else was asleep, the close-packed houses shut up and silent. The children hurried past them and turned down Cupmakers' Street.

At the far end, the darkness was broken by a pool of light. They ran towards it. The light was shining from their own little house. The door was wide open, flooding the ground in front with lamplight. And...their father was standing in front of it!

'Pa!' cried Dalla running into his arms, 'you're home!'

'Where have you three been?' cried Snorri in a fury. 'We've only been gone a few days and here you are, running around town in the middle of the night like a pair of ruffians and a shameless floozy! Aki, I thought I could trust you to look after the other two, but you've let me down terribly! You wicked boy. I'll give you all a whipping.'

'But Pa,' said Dalla, 'we've been up the palace. Do you like my new dress and apron and jewels? And look: I've got some gold!'

Thora came bustling out. Even in the lamplight, they could see that her face was red from crying.

'You bad girl!' she cried. 'I've been worried sick about you! I suppose you led the boys into trouble, did you? And what's that in your hand? A gold coin? Oh Dalla, no! Where did you steal that from? And that smart dress?!'

'I didn't steal anything!' protested Dalla.

'It's true,' said Aki, 'she got them honestly, Mam. Queen Gunnhild gave them to her. And we've both got some gold from the King. And look at our clothes too!'

'Queen Gunnhild?!' cried Thora. 'The King? What's this nonsense about?'

'They're our reward, Mam,' said Frodi, 'for killing

their arch-enemy. He was a berserk, which was bad enough. Only he was even worse. He was...'

'Kill?' cried Thora. 'A berserk? Our Dalla didn't get involved in that, I hope? Girls shouldn't...'

Dalla clamped her mouth shut. *Don't tell!* she thought. *Queen Gunnhild said I mustn't tell anyone about the poison.*

'Kill who?' said Snorri.

'It was this evil man. He disguised himself as a berserk,' said Aki. 'And Pa, it turned out he was really that wicked child-killer, you know, Grim Gruesome!'

'Honestly, Aki!' scolded Thora. 'That's the sort of daft story Dalla would make up. Grim Gruesome isn't real, you know. He's just a silly tale all parents tell to frighten their children into being good. I thought you and Frodi at least were old enough to realise that.'

'That's what King Eirik and Queen Gunnhild said too,' said Dalla.

'But when people started talking about him in the marketplace,' said Frodi, 'most of the adults said they believed in him.'

Aki nodded.

'Anyway, we *saw* him,' said Dalla. 'Oh Mam, Pa, he was horrible! A monster! He put spells on Aki and

173

Frodi with his finger-stump!'

Thora shook her head sceptically.

But Snorri said thoughtfully, 'Mind you, if by any chance it *was* true, that would explain it.'

'Explain what?' said Frodi.

'Why we were called away on a wild goose chase,' said Snorri. 'You know that rune message your Mam got, saying your Aunty Jorunn was dying? Well, it turned out to be a fake. After travelling all that way over the hills, when we got to her farm, we found her completely well. She was astonished to see us. So just supposing Grim Gruesome were real: it could have been him who sent that message. You know, to get us out of the way after he'd picked out you three to be his victims!'

'Honestly, Snorri!' sighed Thora. 'Now you're talking like a fanciful child yourself!'

'All right,' said Snorri sheepishly. 'But let's keep an open mind, eh? Now, did you boys say you killed a villain? Well, well, well! Fancy my own sons doing such a great deed at such a tender age! Astonishing! I knew you were both brave lads but...heroes already! I can't take it in.'

'Dalla was there too,' said Aki.

'She was very brave,' said Frodi.

Dalla smiled secretly to herself. She thought, *If only they knew!*

'Come on,' said Thora. 'Why are we all standing out here in the cold? And the noise we're making! The neighbours will all be poking their noses in if we're not careful. Let's get inside.'

They followed her into the house. All the lamps were burning brightly and there was a roaring fire. They sat round it for a while, telling each other about their adventures. Then they all snuggled down under blankets on the wall-benches to go to sleep.

'Mam, Pa,' said Dalla suddenly, 'I haven't told you the most exciting thing yet.'

'What exciting thing?' said Thora sleepily. 'Hurry up, Dalla, I'm exhausted, what with our long journey and then all the upset of getting home and finding you lot missing.'

'You tell them, Aki,' said Dalla. 'If *I* try, they'll just accuse me of telling fibs.'

Frodi nudged Aki and sniggered.

'Well just listen to this,' said Aki. 'Like I told you, Queen Gunnhild seems to have taken a real liking to our Dalla.'

'You're joking,' said Thora.

'I swear on Thor and Odin that I'm not,' said Aki. 'This is completely true, Mam. Not only did the Queen give Dalla that piece of gold – but she's also asked her to be her serving maid!'

'What?!' said Snorri. 'Our naughty Dalla? You really are making this up!'

'He's not,' said Frodi.

'But that's impossible!' said Thora. 'Doesn't Queen Gunnhild realise that she's the laziest, most disobedient girl in Jorvik?'

'Not any more I'm not,' said Dalla smugly. 'I don't mind being good for the Queen!'

38

Dalla started work at Jorvik Palace the very next day. She had to hang up Queen Gunnhild's dresses, polish her jewellery and comb her hair. To everyone's surprise, she got on really well. In fact, the Queen declared Dalla was her favourite maid and even trusted her with important secrets.

Snorri and Thora almost burst out of their skins with relief and pride. They couldn't believe the change in their wayward daughter.

However, before Aki and Frodi got the chance to join the King's army, King Eirik was killed in a battle. The Viking kingdom came to an end and Jorvik was seized by the King of England.

Queen Gunnhild fled across the sea to Denmark. She took her favourite maid with her. And Dalla begged and nagged the Queen, until she agreed to let

Aki and Frodi join her band of bodyguards.

So all three of Snorri and Thora's children ended up living with nobles!

But that's not quite the end of this story. For unfortunately, the battle in the forest didn't really succeed in ridding the North Lands of Grim Gruesome.

It was all King Eirik's fault. If only he had believed that the berserk was really Grim Gruesome in disguise! Then he would have ordered his soldiers to bury or burn his body straight away. But as you know, they left it out in the forest overnight – and that was a big mistake.

For when they returned to the hideout the next day, the body had vanished!

And strange marks had appeared all around. Some were in the soil outside the ruined house; some were inside the room where Aki had been imprisoned. The old fire-pit had been turned upside down, as if someone had been scrabbling through it.

New rumours spread around Jorvik like wildfire. It didn't take much to convince people that the berserk was really Grim Gruesome – and that he hadn't been killed properly after all. The rumours claimed that the twitching of his body wasn't death-tremors, but a struggle to keep himself alive. Soon it was common knowledge that Grim had been poisoned – though nobody guessed who had done it.

Did Grim himself realise what had happened? Did he know ancient secrets of healing magic?

Did he crawl to the broken door of the ruined house, clamber through it and scrabble in the fire-pit for black lumps of charcoal? Did he swallow the charcoal, knowing it would absorb the poison and slowly cure him?

A few days later, people living in the plains outside Jorvik saw a gigantic man in a billowing cloak, galloping up the road on a silver-maned horse. He was heading northwards, towards the wild hills of Scotland.

On his way, this man claimed a traveller's rights, forcing people to take him in to their firesides, to give him a meal and a bed for the night. He always kept his face hidden under a deep hood. His hosts shuddered at the evil stench that hung about him and recoiled from his festering finger-stump and his burn-blistered arm. Even worse, every cup that he drank from was left with a revolting black stain where his mouth had touched it.

And so the dread of Grim Gruesome spread even further through the North Lands. Before long he was spinning another web of evil. But I can't tell you about it now – for that's another grim and gruesome story!

'Wolf-guts! Whale-doom! This I swear:
I'll stalk vile children everywhere.
I'll snatch and spike them in my snare
and boil their bones in dark despair!'

King Eirik Blood-Axe and Queen Gunnhild
were real people, who ruled over Jorvik
(modern York) and the Viking kingdom in England
in the middle of the 10th Century.
You can find out more about them in the
'Gruesome Facts and Fun' section of
www.grimgruesome.com

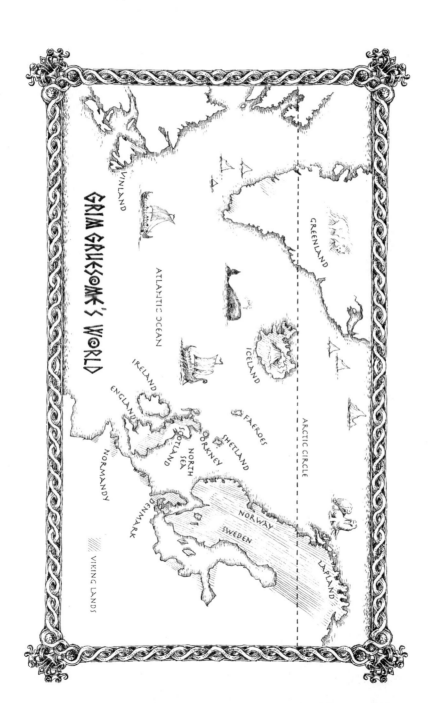

GRIM GRUESOME
VIKING VILLAIN

THE CURSED SWORD

ISBN: 978-0-9537454-3-2

Bjarni desperately needs a sword so he can join a pirate ship and win some treasure, but he can't afford to buy one. Then Astrid's mysterious, long-lost uncle appears out of the blue and offers to lend him one.

This sword is fantastic but it's carved with strange rune letters which turn out to be a dangerous curse. As soon as Bjarni tries fighting with it, he and Astrid plunge into a terrifying adventure with bloodthirsty pirates and a mysterious fortune teller – leading them straight into the clutches of the evil Grim Gruesome!

Look out
for the third Grim Gruesome book,

TROLLS' TREASURE

coming early in 2010.

It's another thrilling adventure
set in a sea-washed Viking island realm
and crammed with
mystery,
treasure and
sword-fights!

Have you visited
the Grim Gruesome website yet?

go to:

www.grimgruesome.com

★ Find out more about the Grim Gruesome books!

★ Download colourful bookmark designs!

★ Play the Grim Gruesome board game!

★ Learn interesting facts about the Viking Age!

★ Meet author Rosalind Kerven!